Sober

A Novel Set in the World of Drink

Samfa12

Paperback ISBN: 978-1-7646384-0-1

Hardback ISBN: 978-1-7646384-1-8

Second Edition

Published by Samfa12

Sober: A Novel Set in the World of Drink

Prologue: Hum

The first sound is a hum you can't locate.

Not wind.

Not a voice.

Not an engine.

A steady A/C unit set to warm, doing its quiet, monotonous work. The kind of sound you notice only after it stops.

It runs through the dark like a thin wire.

For a moment nothing else arrives to join it. No footsteps. No doors. Just that low mechanical note filling a space that hasn't revealed itself yet.

The screen is black.

If you stare long enough, you begin to notice your own breathing. The small intake through the nose. The slower release. Fabric shifts when you move your shoulders. A sleeve brushing against a chair. Someone in the distance clearing their throat.

The hum stays constant.

Somewhere far away, traffic passes. Not loud enough to interrupt the sound, just a brief rise in the background, then gone again. A vehicle slowing at a light. A door shutting. The faint bark of a dog carried between buildings.

The hum continues as if none of that matters.

Then light comes in like a door opening to a lit room.

Not bright.

Just enough to show what is there.

Shapes arrive slowly.

A counter first. The flat line of it cutting the room into front and back. Its surface is clean but worn in the places hands rest most often. A plastic mat lies near the register, its edges curling slightly from years of use.

Behind it, shelves.

Boxes arranged by habit. Small white ones. Larger coloured cartons with brand names printed in careful fonts. Some lean forward slightly where they have been pulled and replaced through the day. Others sit untouched, their edges sharp and even.

A strip of fluorescent light runs above them.

It flickers once, barely noticeable, before settling into a steady glow. The tubes buzz softly, a thin electrical note layered over the hum of the A/C.

A woman stands behind the register.

Her hair is tied back in a braid that rests against the collar of her coat. A few loose strands have escaped near her temple. She moves them away with the back of her wrist without pausing what she is doing.

Her hands move without hurry.

One hand slides a box from the shelf. The other turns it to read the expiry date printed along the seam. She nods to herself in a way that suggests the number was expected.

The box returns to the shelf facing forward.

Another replaces it.

Turn.

Check.

Return.

The motions are small and practiced. The kind that settle into the body after enough days repeating them.

The hum remains constant.

Near the counter sits a small plastic tray of receipts. A thin fan of paper curls upward from it. One slips loose and slides slightly toward the edge when the air from the vent shifts.

Beside the tray, a pen rests with its cap chewed at the end.

A laminated sign advertises flu shots in three languages.

Somewhere behind the counter, a refrigerator motor kicks on. Its deeper vibration joins the hum for a few seconds before fading again.

Outside the window, the city is already moving.

A bus stops at the curb. The air brakes release with a soft sigh. Two people step down. One checks their phone before walking off. The other adjusts a backpack strap and crosses the street without looking up.

Headlights slide across the glass briefly before continuing down the road.

Inside, the shop remains still.

The woman reaches beneath the counter and lifts a small paper bag. She folds the top once. Then again. Her fingers press the crease flat against the edge of the counter.

Somewhere further down the block, a metal shutter rolls halfway down over a shopfront. The sound carries faintly through the glass. A café worker stacks chairs inside a windowed room. Each chair lands with a hollow tap against the one beneath it.

A cyclist passes.

The wheel spokes flicker under the streetlight like thin silver lines.

Inside the pharmacy, a clock ticks quietly on the wall. The second hand moves in small, deliberate jumps. Each click arrives a moment after the last.

The woman pauses with a box in her hand and looks at the shelf as if confirming something only she would notice.

Then she sets it back.

Her hands rest on the counter for a moment.

Outside, someone laughs. The sound travels halfway down the street before disappearing into traffic.

A car door slams.

A pedestrian pushes through the crosswalk just as the light changes.

The city continues.

The woman adjusts the register drawer so it sits flush with the counter again. Her fingers brush a small scratch in the laminate. She wipes it with the edge of her sleeve even though nothing was there.

The fluorescent light hums overhead.

The A/C unit continues its steady note behind the wall.

Outside the window, the city is already moving.

It does not pause to watch.

Chapter One: Close

Sober checks the expiry dates because it is a kind of prayer that doesn't pretend to be one.

She turns the small cardboard boxes slowly, the motion practiced enough that she does not need to look down every second. A thumb presses the edge of the label. The other hand steadies the stack so nothing tips.

The fluorescent strips above her head buzz faintly. One of them flickers once and settles again.

She reads the date.

October. Fine.

The box turns back to the shelf with its front square to the aisle.

The shop smells faintly of antiseptic and cardboard. Beneath that is something warmer from the street outside. Fried food drifting in each time the door opens.

The rustle of a paper bag comes from the counter.

A receipt printer chatters briefly and then stops.

The door chime rings as someone pushes in from the street.

"Evening," she says warmly, and means it.

The man who enters pauses just inside the door the way regular customers do. Long enough for his eyes to adjust to the shop's white light. Long enough to check the shelf where the cough medicine lives before he even reaches the counter.

Outside the glass, traffic moves through the intersection in a slow cycle of red and green. Headlights slide across the pharmacy floor in narrow bands before disappearing again.

The man steps up to the counter and leans on it with his forearms. His jacket is half zipped. One shoelace hangs loose.

A regular customer leans on the counter with a familiarity that has never once crossed into entitlement. He gives her a lopsided smile like he's borrowing it for a moment.

"It's getting chilly out there," he mutters. "Busy?"

"It's been steady," she says, which is her way of saying she can do it. She lifts a small paper packet and taps it once. "Same thing?"

He watches the packet like it might contain better news than it ever has.

"Yeah."

Behind him the door chime rings again. A woman comes in carrying a child on one hip. The child's face is flushed. The woman moves toward the cold medicine aisle and begins reading labels with the quick concentration of someone who does not have time to do it twice.

The man looks past Sober at the shelves, as if the answer might be different tonight. Then he sighs through his nose.

"Kids are sick. I'm sleeping in the hallway again."

"Sorry," she says, and she is.

She places the packet into a small paper bag and folds the top neatly. The receipt prints. She tears it free and slides it across the counter.

She hands him the packet and adds, quietly, "Rest when you can."

He accepts it the way people accept small kindnesses when they have learned not to ask for big ones.

"You too."

He steps aside to let the woman with the child approach the counter.

The child coughs once, a small dry sound. Sober reaches for a bottle behind her without needing to look at the shelf number.

The door chime sounds again. Another face, another need.

A man in work boots walks straight to the painkillers.

A teenager lingers by the cosmetics rack pretending to read ingredients.

A city outside the glass, and the shop as a small warm pocket inside it.

Sober moves between the counter and the shelves with quiet efficiency. She answers questions that repeat every night.

"Two tablets."

"With food if you can."

"Yes, that one's fine."

She prints receipts. She scans barcodes. She folds bags.

The fluorescent lights hum the entire time.

She likes the work because it has edges.

Things come in.

Things go out.

Problems small enough to fit inside a packet.

At the end of the shift, the shop empties slowly rather than all at once.

The teenager leaves without buying anything.

The woman with the child thanks her twice and disappears back into the streetlight.

The man with the work boots counts coins into his palm and nods once before walking out.

The door chime rings one last time.

Then it stops.

The quiet that follows is not silence. The refrigerator unit beneath the counter vibrates gently. Traffic moves through the intersection outside. Somewhere down the street a bus brakes with a soft hydraulic sigh.

Sober counts the till.

Notes in one stack, coins in another.

The coins make a soft metal sound as they touch the counter. She straightens them into rows before sliding them into the drawer.

She writes the number down in the ledger with a pen that scratches faintly across the page.

She checks it twice without drama.

The clock on the wall clicks forward.

She closes the ledger and sets it back in the drawer behind the counter.

On the wall behind her, the clock's second hand clicks like a small metronome. It keeps time no matter what she is thinking.

She turns off the aisle lights one row at a time.

Each switch darkens another shelf.

Boxes fade into shadow. Labels disappear.

The shop becomes smaller.

When the last customer leaves, she flips the sign to CLOSED.

The letters sit in the window like a boundary that doesn't need an explanation.

Outside, the streetlights have already turned on.

Pools of warm and cold light overlap on the pavement. A bus sighs at the curb and pulls away. Its doors close with a soft mechanical clap.

Someone laughs down the block.

The sound is bright for a second before distance and traffic swallow it.

Sober locks the front door and checks it with her hand, not because she doubts it, but because the motion tells her she is done.

The metal handle is cool beneath her fingers.

She turns the key in her pocket as she walks, a small weight.

The city is dark, but not empty.

People pass with grocery bags and takeaway containers. Steam drifts from a noodle shop doorway. A delivery driver idles at the curb scrolling his phone.

A couple argue softly at a pedestrian crossing, words clipped and intimate.

A cyclist rings a bell and threads between bodies.

She nods at a woman outside the kebab shop, and the woman nods back.

A small-town warmth inside a big place that pretends it doesn't have one.

Sober cuts through a side street where the buildings sit closer together.

Brick walls. Old paint peeling near the drains. A narrow strip of sky above.

The air smells faintly of damp concrete.

In an alcove beside a closed café, a cat watches her.

It is thin in the way city animals often are: not starving, but alert, made of muscle and caution.

Its ears tilt forward.

Its tail flicks once.

Sober slows without thinking.

She crouches, not all the way down, just enough to be smaller.

The cat doesn't move closer.

It doesn't run, either.

A car passes at the end of the street. Its headlights slide briefly across the bricks and then disappear.

She holds out her fingers.

The cat sniffs the air, then steps forward in a delicate line, as if every paw placement matters.

When its head reaches her hand, it presses in with a suddenness that surprises her.

His fur is rough, warmed by his own small body.

Sober's throat tightens in a way she doesn't let show on her face.

She scratches behind his ear.

He leans harder, then stops and looks back toward the street as if remembering himself.

"You're not mine."

The words come out the way she says most things: plain, without ornament.

The cat blinks at her, slow and unimpressed.

Then it rubs its cheek once more against her knuckles before stepping back.

"Okay," she whispers, though she doesn't know what she's agreeing to.

She stands.

She brushes her palms on her coat and keeps walking.

The cat watches her go.

She feels that gaze on her back for longer than she should.

In her apartment, she kicks off her shoes and leaves them where they land.

The place is small.

A lamp with a warm shade.

A plant by the window that stubbornly stays alive.

A stack of books she means to read again.

The A/C hum here is quieter than the shop's, but it is the same kind of sound.

Work and home stitched together by a machine's steady breath.

She heats leftovers.

The microwave turns slowly. A plastic lid rattles once against the bowl.

She eats standing at the counter.

Fork scraping lightly against ceramic.

She turns on the TV for noise and does not watch it.

On the counter sits a landline phone.

It is an old habit she has not given up.

A tether.

A number that doesn't change when everything else does.

She washes her bowl.

Water runs.

The dish rack clinks softly.

She dries her hands and stands in the kitchen light for a moment longer than necessary.

The refrigerator hums.

Somewhere outside a car door slams.

Then she turns off the lamp.

The apartment becomes a dim box above the street.

Chapter Two: Metal Chairs

The meeting room smells like instant coffee and someone's deodorant trying too hard.

The smell sits low in the air, caught in the heat of too many bodies and a wall heater that clicks now and then without seeming to help. There is another smell under it too. Wet fabric. Old carpet. Dust from the blinds. The kind of room that gets used for everything and belongs fully to nothing.

Metal chairs scrape against linoleum.

The sound comes in bursts as people arrive in ones and twos, shifting chairs into a circle that is never quite round. Some people sit straight away. Others stand beside their chair for a few seconds first, jacket still on, hands in pockets, as if staying half ready to leave.

Drink comes in with the others and takes the first empty chair that lets him avoid the middle.

People sit in a loose circle, jackets on their laps, hands clasped or spread open on knees. The fluorescent lights turn everyone's skin the same pale colour, as if it is easier not to notice differences here.

Someone coughs into their sleeve.

Someone else tears open a sachet of sugar with their teeth.

A woman near the urn pours hot water into a paper cup and watches the steam rise as if it gives her something to do with her face.

On one wall there are faded posters held up with blu-tack. Community numbers. Crisis lines. A flyer about tenancy advice with one corner curling away from the plaster. Another about quitting smoking. Another about volunteering at a food bank. They have all been there long enough to fade together into a kind of wallpaper.

Near the door a plastic table holds a tin of instant coffee, long life milk, a sleeve of paper cups, a dented urn, and a plate of supermarket biscuits no one touches at first.

Drink keeps his eyes on the floor until it's his turn.

The carpet is threadbare in the centre, worn by years of feet shifting in the same patterns. There are darker marks where chair legs have dug in. A stain near the far side of the room that looks like old tea. Drink notices a loose carpet thread near his shoe. He hooks it once with the sole of his boot, then stops himself.

People keep coming in.

An older man in a hi-vis jacket lowers himself into a chair with care and rubs one knee absent-mindedly. A woman with short hair and tired eyes takes off her raincoat and folds it twice before putting it over the back of her chair. A younger gentleman in office clothes keeps checking his phone until he notices no one else is and slides it face down into his pocket. A woman near the window presses both hands around a paper cup even after it has stopped steaming.

No one looks surprised to see anyone else. That seems to be part of the point.

A man by the urn says quietly to the guy in office clothes, "First time?"

The gentleman glances up, caught, then nods once. "Yeah."

The other man shrugs like that explains enough. "Tea's worse than the coffee."

He almost smiles.

Drink watches that without lifting his head much. Small talk here has no performance to it. No one is trying to charm anyone. They are just filling the room enough to stay in it.

At the front of the circle, if there is a front, a woman with reading glasses opens a notebook and writes the date in neat block letters. She does not call the room to order. She only waits until enough people have sat down that the scraping stops on its own.

Outside, a car door slams. It sounds close, then goes away.

From somewhere down the hall comes the muffled burst of children's voices, then a door shutting, then quiet again. Another group in another room. Another use for the building.

Drink shifts in his chair.

The metal frame gives a small complaint beneath him. Cold comes through the seat even through denim. The room itself is warm in the wrong way, trapped and stale, but the chair keeps its own temperature.

He rubs his palms against his jeans and feels the fabric catch.

The woman with the notebook says, "Alright," in a voice too plain to be called gentle. People settle by a fraction.

There are no opening speeches. No dramatic pause. No atmosphere to build. The room is what it is already.

A man two seats over clears his throat and says, "I'm Mark," and the group answers in a chorus that doesn't lift into anything like joy.

"Hi, Mark."

Mark nods once and keeps his eyes on his shoes while he talks. He speaks about losing half a Saturday and not remembering where it went. About waking up in a parked car with the radio still on. About buying petrol station water and pretending that counted as a plan. His words are blunt. No flourish. The room takes them without flinching.

Another voice follows. "I'm Leanne."

"Hi, Leanne."

Leanne tucks a piece of hair behind one ear, though it slips loose again almost immediately. She talks about hiding bottles in the laundry basket because no one checks the laundry basket. About promising herself she would stop after one glass and hearing herself think it in the same tone every time. About not trusting that tone anymore.

Drink listens because there is nowhere else to put his attention.

Someone else goes next. A truck driver by the sound of him. Then the younger office guy, who speaks too fast for the first few sentences and then slows down when no one interrupts him. A woman near the heater says almost nothing at all, just enough to count as speaking. No one seems bothered by the size of anyone's share. The room is not keeping score that way.

When it reaches him, Drink's tongue sticks for a second.

His hands are damp. He rubs his palms against his jeans and feels the fabric catch.

He looks up because he has to.

The faces are tired, and that tiredness is not a performance. It makes him feel less special, which is almost a relief.

"My name's Lincoln."

He pauses.

"I drink."

The word drops into the circle and sits there. A name and a confession at once.

"Hi, Lincoln," they say, and the sound is polite and unforced, like a door being held open.

He swallows. "I'm trying."

No one claps. No one tells him he's brave. A woman across from him nods once as if to say: *good. Keep going. That's all.*

His voice is already gone again by the time the next person starts. He is grateful for that. Grateful not to have to manage whatever might come out if he kept talking.

He drops his gaze back to the floor and his mind focuses on the coldness of the chair.

A cup is set down on the linoleum near the urn. The tiny sound carries oddly well.

A biscuit packet crinkles.

Someone's keys jingle once, then fall still.

He listens to other stories.

People talk about mornings they don't remember and phone calls they can't undo. They talk about the quiet moment before the first drink, when the mind makes a plan that feels like permission.

A man with paint under his fingernails says he has started avoiding the servo near his place because the drive-through bottle-o sits right beside the pumps. The older man in hi-vis says nothing for a while, then says he has become too good at sounding normal on the phone. A woman by the window says she keeps pouring orange juice first so she can tell herself the glass started clean.

The details vary. The shape underneath them does not.

Drink feels each one land in him and fail to make him feel unique. It is humiliating in a way that helps.

For a moment the room tilts into an older memory.

A schoolyard. Summer heat in the bark chips under the playground tree. Laurel sitting beside him on the swing, both of them too old for it but pretending not to notice.

The chain on his swing had been warm from the sun. Someone had carved initials into the trunk behind them. A magpie had hopped near the lunch tables, head tilted, looking for dropped food. Laurel had her sleeves rolled up and a half-smile she was trying not to let become a grin.

Someone on the oval sings the rhyme under their breath.

Lincoln and Laurel sitting in a tree.

He can't remember who started it. Only that Laurel laughed first, and the laugh made the teasing useless.

The memory fades before the next line can arrive.

The room comes back in pieces.

Fluorescent hum.

Someone clearing their throat.

A spoon stirring instant coffee in a paper cup, the small papery scrape of it.

Drink shifts again and clasps his hands together to stop them moving.

The woman with the notebook says, “Thanks,” to someone who has just finished talking about missing his daughter’s birthday lunch because he was too hungover to drive and too ashamed to explain. She says it the same way she said it to the others. Not more serious. Not less. Consistency is its own kind of mercy.

Drink notices that no one gives advice unless asked. No one leans in. No one tries to solve anyone else. They sit. They speak. They leave room.

A man across the circle reaches for a biscuit at last, breaks it cleanly in half, eats one half, and puts the other back on the plate before seeming to realise that is not how plates work. He takes it again. No one comments.

The heater clicks and keeps failing to become warm enough.

Someone’s wet shoes leave marks on the floor near the door.

A bus goes past outside and the windows shake very slightly in their frames.

Drink doesn’t speak again. He does not trust his voice not to shake. He sits through the hour and counts it as something done.

He counts the room in other ways too.

Three more names.

Two coughs from the same corner.

The woman with the raincoat looking at her watch only once near the end.

The office guy finally drinking his coffee cold because he forgot it was there.

Mark rubbing the side of his thumb over a wedding ring that isn't on his hand anymore.

At some point a late arrival comes in, nods apology to the room without words, and takes a chair from the stack against the wall. The chair legs scream briefly over the linoleum. Nobody flinches. The circle widens half an inch and absorbs him.

Drink sits with his knees apart and his shoulders slightly folded in, a posture old enough to feel structural. He tries once to relax his jaw and discovers it has been clenched the whole time.

The fluorescent light nearest the window flickers once. The room does not react. It must do that often.

At the end there is no big closing note. No crescendo. The woman with the notebook thanks everyone for coming, mentions next week in the same room, same time, and asks someone to leave the cups by the sink.

That is all.

When the meeting ends, chairs scrape back.

The sound is louder than before because people are less careful now that the formal part is over. Metal on frayed carpet and linoleum. A brief chorus of leaving.

People stand in small knots, not friends, but witnesses.

Someone refills the coffee pot.

Someone else folds up pamphlets and stacks them neatly as if order will help.

A man in the hi-vis jacket says to Mark, "See you next week," and the words sound like they have been said before. Leanne asks the woman with the notebook if there are any spare bus tickets in the office drawer like last time. The office guy hovers by the urn, unsure whether to leave fast or slow.

Drink stands because everyone else is standing.

For a second he nearly goes straight for the door. The reflex is clean and strong. Leave before anyone can talk to you. Leave before staying becomes another kind of exposure.

Instead, he waits long enough to let the first cluster pass.

A woman brushing crumbs off her coat glances at him and says, "You came."

He looks at her, unsure if it needs an answer.

She shrugs. "That's something."

Then she picks up her bag and goes.

Near the door there is a table with pens chained to string and a sign-up sheet for volunteers to bring long-life milk next week. Drink looks at the sheet without reading the names. Someone has written in looping blue ink. Someone else in all caps.

A man by the sink rinses out two mugs that don't match the paper cups and leaves them upside down on a tea towel. Another person empties a bin that is mostly full of sugar wrappers and tissues.

Normal tasks. End-of-room tasks. It unsettles Drink how much comfort there is in seeing people clean up after a thing instead of pretending the thing was larger than life.

Outside the community centre, the night is sharper.

Air that feels like it has been rinsed.

Streetlights bleach the pavement. Water left from earlier rain sits in the cracks of the gutter and turns white under the lamps. Somewhere nearby a train horn sounds, distant enough to feel like weather.

Across the road, a pub glows warm and amber through its windows.

The glass throws back a softened version of the room inside. Golden light. Moving shoulders. Raised hands. A television above the bar showing sport without sound from here. Every time the door opens, the hum of conversation leaks out. A laugh bursts, bright and careless, and then the door swings shut again.

Drink stops on the curb.

The pub is a threshold that knows his name without speaking it.

He can smell it even from here when the wind moves right. Beer and fried food and old timber and sweetness gone slightly stale. Familiar enough that his body starts answering before his mind does. Tongue. Hands. Chest. A small quickening everywhere at once.

His sponsor steps up beside him.

A steady man in a plain jacket, hands in pockets, eyes not looking at the pub, not pretending it isn't there.

He stands with his weight even on both feet, like someone who has learned not to lean toward or away from things more than necessary.

"You need a plan."

The sentence is not advice. It's a fact, like weather.

Drink lets out a breath he didn't know he was holding. He stares at the pub door until the warm light begins to ache behind his eyes.

"I know," he says.

A group of three people come out of the pub laughing, one of them already halfway through a story, one holding a cigarette he forgot to light. They move around Drink and his sponsor without noticing them much. The pub door opens wider for a second and the heat from inside touches the cold air, then closes again.

The sponsor looks at him now, not stern, not kind. Just present. "What are you doing tonight?"

Drink's mind reaches for the old answer.

The easy answer.

The answer shaped like relief.

His mouth almost opens on it. He can feel how simple it would be to let the night collapse into its oldest shape.

He forces something else out. “Not home.”

The sponsor nods once, as if that is enough to start with. “Good. Coffee?”

They cross under the streetlight while traffic waits and doesn’t care who they are.

The fast food café is open because it is always open.

Its windows are bright in the flat way of places built to keep you awake rather than welcome. The floor tiles shine with a recent mop. Plastic chairs and sticky tables. A fryer hum that competes with the fluorescent hum overhead. The smell of salt and old oil. Tomato sauce. Cleaning spray. Burnt coffee. The kind of place where you can sit as long as you want because no one expects you to belong.

A teenager in a visor takes orders without looking up much.

A family with two overtired kids occupies a corner booth in a fog of chips and wrappers.

A delivery rider in a wet jacket waits by the pickup screen staring at nothing.

Drink orders a black coffee and watches the cup fill.

The machine spits and hisses. Dark liquid runs into paper. Steam lifts up sharp and bitter. The smell is honest enough to be almost medicinal.

His sponsor orders the same.

They take their cups to a table by the window, one that wobbles until the sponsor slides a sugar sachet under one leg without comment. Cars pass in bright slices. Red lights stop them outside. Green sends them on again. A woman in a uniform wipes down tables with a rag that has seen better days. She works around them without making them feel hurried.

Drink wraps both hands around his cup even though it is too hot yet.

His sponsor stirs his coffee even though it has no sugar.

The spoon clicks the side of the cup. A small repeating sound.

"My wife," the sponsor says suddenly, staring at the table, "she used to do this thing. She'd leave the porch light on even if I wasn't home. Like it was a promise."

Drink waits.

He has learned not to fill silences too quickly. Silences are where the truth lives, if you don't chase it away.

Around them the café keeps happening.

A machine beeps behind the counter until someone presses the right button.

One of the tired kids starts crying because his chips are touching the sauce.

The delivery rider's number flashes on the screen and he stands without expression.

"She's gone now," the sponsor continues, and his voice stays flat, as if he's reading from a label. "I still catch myself thinking she'll be there when I open the door. Like… like I can earn it back."

Drink feels the words land somewhere tender.

He wants to say, *I know that feeling.*

Instead, he just nods.

Outside the window, a bus kneels at the curb and rises again. A man in business clothes jogs the last few steps and still misses it. He throws one hand out in frustration, then drops it, already defeated.

A long pause.

The sponsor's spoon clicks against the cup, a small sound repeating.

"She's not dead," the sponsor says quietly, and the confession changes the air. "She left. Took the kids. Took the house. I tell people she's gone because it's easier than saying I did it to myself."

Drink's throat tightens.

In his mind, the pub's warm glow flares and dims like a heartbeat.

The sponsor looks up then, meeting Drink's eyes for the first time tonight. "You don't get to trade honesty for comfort, mate. Not here."

Drink nods again, because it is all he can manage without breaking apart in the middle of a café that smells like grease.

He drinks the coffee too soon and burns his tongue. The sting helps.

Neither of them pretends the conversation fixed anything. That helps too.

They sit until the cups are half empty and the table has gathered a ring of condensation under one of them. The woman with the rag comes past and wipes the next table over in practiced circles. At the counter someone asks for extra salt. The fryer hums like machinery on a ship.

Later, on the walk back, the streets feel emptier without being empty.

Shops on the strip have pulled down their shutters. A convenience store still burns white with light. Lotto signs. Powerball poster. Refrigerators lined up along the back wall like glowing doors.

The payphone is tucked beside the convenience store, half-forgotten in a city that has moved on to better machines. Its plastic hood is scratched. The metal plate below the numbers has worn smooth in places from hands that had nowhere else to go.

The sponsor points to it.

"Call someone who matters," the sponsor says.

Drink's fingers curl into his palm. "I can't."

"You can."

"I'm not great with self-control," Drink says.

The sponsor shrugs.

"Try force."

Drink looks at him.

For a second it almost feels like a joke.

A tired, sideways kind of joke. Not enough to make the night lighter. Just enough to stop it becoming sacred.

"Yeah," Drink says. "I'll start small."

A man leaves the convenience store with a frozen pizza under one arm and doesn't look their way. A car rolls past slowly with music leaking through closed windows. Somewhere down the block a bottle goes into a bin with a hollow glass knock.

Drink walks across the street like he's walking into a cold room.

He lifts the receiver.

It is heavier than he expects, and the cord twists like a tether.

The plastic smells faintly of rain and old hands. The metal coin slot is scratched around the edges. The booth light above him hums softly, attracting moths that knock themselves stupid against the casing.

He drops coins into the slot with a shaking hand.

They fall louder than they should.

He dials a number he knows by muscle memory.

Each press of the button feels too hard, then not hard enough. He nearly misdials on the last digit and stops to begin again from the start because he does not trust correction tonight.

The line clicks open.

His heart stutters once.

He hears a ring.

Another.

Another.

He stares through the scratched plastic of the booth at his reflection layered over the street beyond. Pale face. Tired eyes. A man using a machine older than his excuses.

When the voice answers, soft with sleep, he forgets everything he planned to say.

"Hi."

Chapter Three: The Call

The landline rings in a way her mobile never does.

It is louder. Sharper. More certain of its right to interrupt. A sound from an older part of the world, when calls arrived inside houses and not inside pockets. It cuts through the apartment cleanly, through the A/C hum, through the dim shape of furniture, through the kind of sleep that never goes very deep.

Sober's eyes open in the dark.

For a second she does not know where she is. The room is all outline. Window. Couch. Table. The lamp on the crate beside the bed. The folded jumper over the chair. A strip of streetlight pressing faintly through the gap in the curtain.

The A/C hum fills the silence like a held breath.

The phone rings again.

She lies still for one beat too long, listening.

The sound seems louder the second time. Or closer.

She pushes herself upright, the sheet slipping to her waist. The cotton drags over her knees. Her hair falls across one side of her face and she brushes it back with the heel of her hand. The apartment is cool except where sleep has warmed the bed.

She reaches for the lamp.

Light snaps on, warm and small.

The room arranges itself around her. The mug in the sink. The book left open face-down on the couch. The folded jumper on the chair that she never puts away. Her shoes near the door, not quite side by side. A receipt on the counter from milk and bread and cat food she no longer buys. A tea towel hanging crooked from the oven handle.

The phone rings a third time, and her stomach drops before her mind catches up.

She knows before she knows.

Not certainty. Not logic. Just recognition moving faster than thought.

She swings her legs off the bed and stands.

The floorboards are cold beneath her bare feet. She crosses the room carefully, each step measured, as if noise might somehow change who is on the other end. The cord of the lamp trails shadow across the floor. The phone sits on the kitchen counter exactly where it always sits. Cream plastic gone slightly yellow with age. Curled cord. A machine that belongs to habits rather than fashion.

It rings again as she reaches for it.

She lifts the receiver and holds it to her ear.

A pause.

Nothing at first except the line's faint electrical hush. Somewhere far off, a small crackle. The city under everything.

Then a voice, hesitant and too familiar. "Hi."

Sober closes her eyes.

In the darkness behind her eyelids, the past is not a montage. It is a hallway. A bedroom. A kitchen. A cat bowl. Silence after a fight. Silence after apologies that stopped meaning anything. A glass left on a windowsill. Shoes kicked off in the wrong place. The smell of stale beer under deodorant. The careful sound of someone trying not to wake the person they have already disappointed.

Her hand tightens on the receiver until her knuckles ache.

She opens her eyes again and looks at nothing. The cupboard door. The chipped handle. The shadow of the drying rack on the wall.

"It's late."

The line is thin. She can hear him breathing on the other end, as if he's afraid any sound will break it.

Beyond that there are smaller sounds. Traffic somewhere near him. A distant engine. The hollow space around a public phone. Wind maybe. Or just the line making everything sound colder than it is.

"I know," he says.

She leans one hip against the counter because standing still is easier if something holds part of your weight. Her free hand flattens against the laminate. It is cool and slightly sticky where she missed a spot after wiping it earlier.

She swallows.

The words she has practised for months come up, steady and bitter at the same time. Not rehearsed exactly. Worn smooth from use inside her own head.

"You shouldn't call."

A small sound from him, not quite a sob, not quite a laugh. Something that begins in one shape and fails to decide on another.

"I just… I needed to—"

"No," she says, and her voice is softer than she expects, which makes it harder. "You can't do this to me."

The silence between them is full.

It is not empty. It is packed with all the times he promised and then didn't. All the times she waited for a version of him that only appeared for a night and then vanished again. Packed with the older geometry of them. Who reached. Who retreated. Who cleaned up. Who slept badly listening for a key in the door.

Outside the window, a car passes through wet streetlight and keeps going.

She looks down at her bare feet on the floorboards and feels how steady they are. Toes flat. Knees unlocked. Weight balanced. This is her life now. It has edges.

On the other end, he does not rush to fill the silence. That almost unsettles her more than pleading would have.

When he speaks again, his voice is roughened down to the grain.

"I'm trying," he says, and the words sound like the meeting room, like fluorescent light, like metal chairs. They sound like something he learned to say because he had to.

Sober's mouth goes dry.

She closes her eyes again, but the dark does not help. The line keeps carrying his breathing into her kitchen. The old habit of listening returns before she wants it to. Listening for what state he is in. Listening for slur, for sway, for the lie that comes too fast, for anger hiding under apology. The old scan flickers through her anyway, automatic as checking stock dates.

He sounds tired.

That is all she lets herself know.

"I have work."

The sentence lands between them with the plainness of a locked door.

On the other end, she hears his breath catch.

For a second she thinks he might beg. She braces for it. Muscles tightening. Jaw setting. Heart angry at itself for still caring enough to prepare.

But he doesn't beg.

The pause stretches. In it she hears a bus sigh at a curb somewhere in the city. Or imagines it. Hears a voice in the far distance near his end of the line. Hears the old building around her settle by a fraction.

"Okay," he says, and it is so small that it almost breaks her anyway.

She turns her head toward the window without really seeing outside. Her reflection is faint in the glass. Lamp light. Tired face. Hair loose and uneven from sleep. A woman standing barefoot in her own kitchen with a phone in her hand and no one here to tell her what kindness should cost.

She waits one more heartbeat, because leaving first is a choice she has earned.

She lets herself feel the weight of it, not as punishment, but as proof that she is still here. That the line between them is a line because she says so. That ending a call can be an action, not a failure.

Then she puts the receiver down.

The plastic settles into its cradle with a small final click.

The dial tone begins immediately, indifferent and steady.

Sober stands in the kitchen light with her hand still on the phone, as if it might ring again and she might need to stop it by sheer will.

It doesn't.

The A/C hum goes on. The fridge motor kicks in. Somewhere in the building a tap knocks once inside a pipe. The apartment resumes its own sounds with no interest in what just passed through it.

She leaves her hand there another second and then lifts it away.

On the counter beside the phone is a folded shopping list with two items crossed out and one left uncrossed because she forgot. Dish soap. She looks at the word as if she has never seen it before.

Outside the window, the city continues.

A siren passes somewhere far away, muted by distance and glass. A car door slams. Someone laughs. The world doesn't hold its breath. Traffic washes and recedes. A set of footsteps goes by under the window and then is gone.

She reaches up and turns off the lamp.

The room falls back into shadow, shaped now by streetlight and appliance glow. The red standby dot on the television. The softer blue from the microwave clock. The window holding the city at a distance.

She goes back to bed.

The sheets are cool where she left them. She slides under them and turns onto her side, facing away from the phone though the apartment is too small for that to mean much. Her hand tucks under the pillow. Then comes out again. Then rests flat on the mattress instead.

Her heart keeps thudding, loud in her ribs, like it is angry at her for being alive.

She stares into the dark.

The ceiling is only barely visible. A pale plane above her. The A/C breathes. Somewhere outside a motorcycle passes, then another quieter car. In the flat upstairs, something scrapes softly across a floor and stops.

She swallows against the dryness in her throat.

The old urge to pick the receiver back up flickers once, not because she wants to speak, but because endings used to be followed by repair. By managing him. By checking. By making sure the damage was not actively spreading. The body remembers roles long after the mind has resigned from them.

She keeps her hands where they are.

In the dark, she whispers into the pillow, not a prayer, not an apology.

"Not again."

The words disappear into fabric. No witness. No ceremony.

After that there is only lying still.

The kind of stillness that is work.

The city keeps moving below. Somewhere, very faint, glass is emptied into a bin. Somewhere a truck changes gears. Somewhere a pedestrian light clicks over for no one she can see.

Eventually the rhythm of the A/C begins to flatten the edges of things.

When she finally sleeps, the hum carries her under like a slow tide.

In the morning, she will open the shop.

She will put the key in the lock before full rush hour and shoulder the door open with her bag still on. She will flick on the lights row by row. The shelves will appear. The counter. The till. The small, neat world of packets and labels and tasks that end when completed.

She will smile at her regulars.

She will stack boxes and count coins and keep the world's small needs moving.

The phone will sit on the counter, silent.

And somewhere across the city, a man will hold a payphone receiver for one second longer than necessary, hearing nothing but the line's flat answer.

Chapter Four: Chain

Drink doesn't walk home.

The payphone is in the next town over, outside a strip of closed shops with roller doors pulled down and graffiti silvered by streetlight. A convenience store glows under harsh fluorescent tubes. Behind it sits the community centre where metal chairs scrape and people say their names like facts. The building is still lit in two windows. Someone inside stacks chairs. Someone rinses mugs in a sink. The world goes on cleaning up after revelation.

When he puts the receiver down, his hand stays there a second longer than it needs to.

Not bargaining. Not praying.

Just refusing to let go of the shape of her voice.

The receiver is cold and slightly greasy from public use. The cord has twisted itself into loops from years of other hands. Above the booth, a tube light hums and draws moths that batter themselves softly against the casing.

Across the road, the pub throws amber light onto the footpath each time the door opens. Laughter comes out in loose bursts. A smoker stands under the awning with one shoulder hunched against the damp. Glass clinks inside. A television flashes blue-white over the bar. No one in there is thinking about him.

The sponsor stands beside him on the footpath, hands in his pockets, looking past the pub like it isn't a magnet.

"You're not going to walk," the sponsor says.

Drink shakes his head.

The road home is too long and too dark. Walking would feel like penance, and he has spent years mistaking pain for progress.

He does not say that aloud. He only shifts his weight and rubs his thumb against the edge of the payphone shelf where old sticker glue has gone hard and ridged.

They wait at the curb.

A taxi rolls up slow, wipers ticking. Tyres hiss on damp bitumen. The driver leans across and unlocks the back door without asking who they are or why they're waiting outside a payphone at this hour. Drink slides into the back seat and gives his address in a voice that tries not to shake.

The sponsor shuts the door for him.

Drink looks up once through the rain-streaked glass. The sponsor lifts two fingers in something smaller than a wave. Then the taxi pulls away.

Inside, the car smells faintly of pine air freshener, stale coffee, and vinyl warmed all day then cooled too fast. The radio murmurs talkback at low volume. Some caller is angry about roadworks. The host makes interested sounds and keeps the segment moving.

Streetlights smear across the side window. The meter ticks up in small increments.

He watches it anyway.

Not because he can't afford it, but because he still expects the world to punish him for wanting anything easy.

At a red light the taxi idles beside the pub strip. A group of young men cross in front of the bonnet, loud with the kind of confidence that comes free with borrowed invincibility. One of them carries takeaway chips. Another is still laughing at something that happened half a block ago. They pass without looking in.

The meter climbs.

Drink rests both hands flat on his thighs to stop himself checking his phone. There is nothing on it. No new message. No correction. No rescue. The seatbelt presses diagonally across his chest. He can feel his own pulse against it.

The driver clears his throat once. "Been a wet week," he says, looking at the road.

Drink nods, then realises the driver can't see that clearly in the mirror. "Yeah."

That is the whole conversation.

The silence returns, practical and welcome.

He pays with his card without checking the balance first.

The machine beeps approval. The simple fact of that feels like a confession.

He has been doing better at work. There is some money. It doesn't make him good. It only means he can get home without pretending he deserves the cold.

The borrowed room smells like detergent and old carpet.

The house is quiet in the way shared houses become late at night. A television murmurs in the living room, turned down low. His roommate coughs once near the kitchen. A tap runs and stops. Something shifts in the fireplace as the last of the wood settles.

Drink unlocks his door and steps inside.

The wall unit hums at once. The A/C hum is a steady breath that makes the quiet feel occupied. It pushes cool air that smells faintly dusty across the room. The lamp beside the bed is off. Light sneaks around the edge of the curtain and lays a pale strip across the carpet.

The room is as he left it.

One wardrobe, closed.

A plastic laundry basket half full of clean clothes he never folded.

A mug with a tea bag gone grey in the bottom.

The small table with coins, keys, a charger, and a packet of aspirin.

The cat is on the bed, curled into the centre of the blanket as if the room belongs to him.

He lifts his head when Drink comes in.

One slow blink.

No greeting. No forgiveness. Just acknowledgement.

Drink closes the door gently behind him and stands there a second, letting the room settle around him. The carrier strap has left a red groove across his palm. He flexes his fingers once. The skin feels stiff.

The cat watches all of this without interest.

Drink sits on the edge of the bed and lets his hands rest on his knees until they stop trembling.

The mattress dips. The cat opens one eye wider, judges the disturbance acceptable, and leaves him alive.

"Alright," he murmurs, because it is the only promise he can make without lying.

The cat stretches, front paws long, claws catching briefly in the blanket. Then he gets up, turns once, and presses his head into Drink's thigh before settling again. A small weight. A boundary that still chooses to stay near.

Drink puts one hand carefully on the cat's back.

The fur is warmer than he expects.

Outside, a car door shuts in the driveway. In the kitchen, a cupboard closes softly. Water moves through the pipes with a quiet rushing sound. The room remains itself.

He does not undress properly. Shoes off. Socks peeled away and left near the bed. Jeans still on. Shirt still on. He lies back without pulling the blanket down and stares at the ceiling where the parking lot light makes a pale shifting square.

Sleep comes in fragments.

In one of them, the phone rings again and again.

Not loudly. Not urgently. Just with the dull persistence of something that knows it will outlast him. He reaches for it in the dream and his hand won't close properly. The cord grows longer each time he tries to pull it closer. Somewhere on the other end, breathing. Then only line noise.

He wakes with his mouth dry and his chest tight.

The A/C is still humming. The cat has moved to his feet. For a second he does not know whether the ringing happened or not. He fumbles for his phone on the table, lights the screen, sees nothing, sets it down again face-up.

He closes his eyes.

In another fragment, the pub door opens on warm light that smells like relief.

Not the bar from tonight exactly. All of them at once. Sticky floor. old timber. damp coasters. the soft chemical bite of spilled beer drying. Someone calling his name from across the room with too much affection to be safe. A glass appearing in his hand before he remembers taking it. The first swallow spreading through him like an instruction.

He wakes before it can finish.

His tongue feels thick. His jaw aches from clenching.

He rolls onto one side and pulls the pillow over part of his face. The fabric smells of laundry powder and sleep that never quite settled in.

Then another fragment.

He is back under the same playground tree.

She is leaning against the trunk, drawing circles in the dirt with the toe of her shoe. The bark behind her shoulder is rough and split. Dry leaves have gathered against the roots. Somewhere nearby a magpie cracks a call across the oval. The afternoon light is yellow in the way school afternoons used to be when the day felt bigger than it was.

She has one hand hooked through the strap of her bag. And is pretending not to smile.

Someone nearby is singing again, the same stupid rhyme that followed them through half of high school.

Lincoln and Laurel sitting in a tree.

K.I.S.S.I.N.G

The voice drifts lazily to the next line.

First comes love.

Drink wakes before the rest of the song can arrive.

He lies very still.

The room is grey now rather than dark. Morning pressing thinly through the curtain. A truck reverses somewhere outside, beeping with bureaucratic patience. His roommate's phone alarm in the next room goes off too long before being slapped quiet.

The cat steps over his shin and sits by the window, looking at the moving brightness at the edge of the curtain.

In the morning, the city is already moving outside the window.

Cars. Footsteps. A radio in the next room, tinny through the wall. A world that does not slow down to see if he's ready.

He sits at the small table and opens his phone.

The screen's light is hard on tired eyes.

There is no address for her. There is only the City, and the job title he can't stop holding like a thread: pharmacist.

He opens maps. Closes it. Opens notes. Closes that too. Opens his contacts and sees old names that belong to versions of him who promised too easily. His thumb hovers over hers for a second, then moves away.

The sponsor's voice sits in his memory, plain and steady.

You need a plan.

Drink knows what he wants to do. A grand gesture. Turning up. Being seen. Standing at a counter and letting her look at him long enough to understand he isn't the same man who called at midnight for rescue.

He also knows what he deserves is not part of the equation.

The city has too many pharmacies.

Three is a number a person can attempt.

He writes three words in his notes app, because a plan has to be small before it can be real.

City. Three pharmacies.

He stares at the line as if it might become less pathetic if he gives it time.

It doesn't.

He can't justify it any other way. If she is a pharmacist in the city, she will be somewhere ordinary, somewhere she can help people, somewhere with shelves and rules and quiet routine.

Corporate chain. Wellness clinic. Hospital.

Three spaces. Three chances to keep walking through the pressure without reaching for relief. He hates himself for thinking in chances, like the universe is a machine that rewards effort.

Still, he needs motion.

Motion is how he survives.

He gets up and fills the cat bowl in the kitchen from the nearly empty packet on the counter. Dry food rattles against ceramic. The cat comes over without hurry, sniffs once, and begins eating with the focus of an animal that has never once confused appetite for morality.

Drink stands there and watches longer than necessary.

Then he fills the kettle and forgets to turn it on.

He notices after a full minute, presses the switch, waits for the click.

He carries the mug back to his room while the kettle begins its slow climb toward boiling. The wall unit keeps humming. The cat keeps eating. Morning keeps happening around him without endorsement.

Before he leaves, he kneels by the bed and looks at the cat.

"I'm taking you," he says quietly, as if he can negotiate.

The cat stands, stretches, and jumps down without hurry. He does not run. He does not follow immediately. He pads to the food bowl, eats a few more bites, then walks to the door and waits there, tail low, as if he's decided the only way out is forward.

Drink exhales once through his nose.

"Yeah," he says. "Fair."

The pet supply shop opens early and smells like rubber toys, dry kibble, cardboard, and shampoo.

It sits beside a tobacconist and a discount phone repair kiosk, all of them sharing the same exhausted awning and sun-faded signage. Inside, fluorescent tubes buzz overhead. Leashes hang in bright rows. Plastic bowls stack inside each other by size. A woman with a pram studies flea treatments with the expression of someone comparing tax policy.

Drink buys a carrier from a shop that sells cheap pet supplies and phone chargers in the same aisle.

The fabric is thin. The zip catches. The handle digs into his palm when he lifts it. There is a cartoon paw print on the tag that makes the whole thing seem flimsier.

At the counter, a young guy with chipped nail polish scans it and says, “Need a receipt?”

Drink nods.

The guy tears it off and puts it in the bag without looking at him again.

The cat sniffs the opening, unimpressed, then steps inside as if he’s doing Drink a favour. Drink closes the zip gently, careful not to turn care into control.

On the train to the City, he sits with the carrier on his lap and watches paddocks become streets, then blocks, then glass and traffic.

The carriage smells faintly of damp coats, takeaway coffee, and old upholstery. A woman in scrubs sleeps upright with her head against the window. Two schoolboys share earbuds and try not to laugh too loudly at something on a phone. An older man reads the racing pages with intense disappointment. The announcement chime cuts through at each station, followed by a voice too calm for the hour.

The cat’s eyes stay open the whole way, alert to every shift in sound.

Now and then the carrier shifts with a quiet repositioning from inside. Drink puts his hand against the mesh once, not enough to trap, just enough to be there. The cat does not lean into it, but he stops moving for a moment.

When they arrive, the air feels different.

Hot concrete. Exhaust. Too many people moving too close.

The station empties into the City in a rush of shoes, bags, coffee cups, expressions already halfway to wherever they need to be. Drink lifts the carrier and lets the crowd carry him forward because choosing to stop would make him disappear.

The corporate chain pharmacy is the first place he tries because it is the easiest to hide in.

A logo designed to look friendly.

Sliding doors that sigh like the building is breathing.

Inside, the light is too bright. Product aisles run in straight lines like rules. Promotional signs shout about discounts and wellness points. The air smells of disinfectant and sweet artificial perfume. A speaker overhead plays music too soft to matter.

Drink takes a basket and walks the aisles as if he belongs.

The plastic handle bites into the crook of his fingers. He keeps the carrier tucked close with the other hand. A mother steers a stroller around him without looking up. A man in a polo shirt compares protein powders with grave concentration. Someone near the scripts counter coughs into a tissue and asks how long antibiotics usually take.

The first pressure is small.

Mouthwash in neat rows, labels bright. Alcohol content tucked into fine print. Bottles that promise cleanliness. A fresh start.

His hand moves before he remembers it's moving.

He stops with his fingers an inch from the plastic.

His mouth tastes like yesterday's coffee and sleep that didn't work. He swallows and reads the label slowly, forcing his eyes to stay on the numbers.

His heart beats faster.

It is ridiculous.

It is real.

He moves on.

Cough syrup. Dark liquid in glass. Thick and medicinal. He can almost taste the heat that would spread through his chest. The thought is not a thought. It is a body memory, vivid and hungry.

He turns away sharply, bumping his basket against the shelf. A row of lozenges shivers in place. A woman in uniform looks at him from the end of the aisle. Her gaze is brief, indifferent, already elsewhere.

Drink's skin prickles anyway.

Shame arrives as fast as craving, as if they travel together.

In the antiseptic aisle, he reads labels the way he used to read timetables. Rules, doses, margins of error. He traces his thumb along the edge of a box and imagines that control is something you can buy in cardboard packaging.

A convex security mirror reflects him in a warped oval. His face looks stretched, unfamiliar. He feels like he's watching someone else shop for a life they haven't earned.

He buys soap and toothpaste and the cheapest vitamins.

The cashier scans each item with the pace of someone on their fifth hour of repetition. Beep. Beep. Beep. The register screen throws blue light across her knuckles. A half-drunk energy drink sits beside the till. A pen on a chain taps the counter when she reaches for it.

He pays with his card and does not make eye contact because he is afraid she might see him.

He hesitates before stepping away from the counter.

"There's something else," he says.

The cashier looks up, already halfway through the next task.

"I'm trying to find someone. A pharmacist."

She waits.

"Laurel."

She thinks for a moment, then shakes her head.

"Not here."

Drink nods once.

"Thanks."

Outside, the air tastes like exhaust and hot concrete.

He sits on a bench near the entrance and holds the paper bag on his lap as if it contains something fragile. Office workers pass with lunch containers and bad shoes. A courier swears softly at a faulty scanner. Two teenagers share a packet of chips and argue about whether to skip class for the rest of the afternoon. Somewhere above street level, construction hammers on metal in short brutal bursts.

He opens his notes app again and adds a small mark beside the first line.

One down.

He thinks of Sober's voice in the dark.

"It's late. You shouldn't call. I have work."

He understands now that the sentences were not punishment.

They were information.

He scrolls through old contacts. Her number is still there, untouched, like a bruise you keep pressing to see if it still hurts.

He doesn't call.

Instead, he opens his notes app and types one line under City.

Three pharmacies.

Do not demand.

He looks at it until the words stop seeming performative and start seeming necessary.

Waiting feels like doing nothing.

Doing nothing feels like dying.

He lifts the carrier onto the bench beside him. The cat's eyes meet his through the mesh. Not forgiving. Not condemning. Just there.

Drink stands up and starts walking again, bag in one hand, carrier in the other. The City moves around him as if he is a normal person doing normal errands.

At the station, he pauses by a bin and sees an unopened mini bottle of something clear, still in its plastic wrap. Someone dropped it, careless, like it meant nothing.

His stomach lurches.

His hands go cold.

He stares at it for too long. Standing still makes the pressure rise. The world narrows. The bottle becomes a point of light. A man brushes past him with a suitcase and mutters, "Sorry." A train announcement blurs overhead. Somewhere nearby a child asks for a snack and is told not now.

He could take it and no one would know.

He imagines the cat watching him.

He imagines Sober's hand on the receiver as she hangs up first.

He imagines his sponsor's flat voice: You don't get to trade honesty for comfort.

Drink takes a step back.

Then another.

He leaves the bottle in the bin.

On the platform, a commuter sits beside him, scrolling on her phone. She wears a high-vis jacket and looks exhausted in the way people look when they have no time for drama.

She glances at the cat carrier. "Yours?"

Drink nods.

"Cute," she says, and then she looks away again, done with the interaction.

A train roars in, wind slapping at Drink's face. The doors open. People spill out. People pour in.

Drink boards with the crowd.

He sits by the window and watches the City slide past, bright shopfronts and dark alleys, warm pools of light and hard fluorescent glare.

He keeps his hands on his knees so they don't reach for anything.

When the train pulls away, the platform vanishes behind him like a choice made and sealed.

He does not feel brave.

He feels tired.

And for now, that is enough.

Chapter Five: The Offer

At midday, Sober's shop smells like hand cream and rain.

The rain has not settled into anything serious. It comes in passing sheets, enough to darken the pavement and send people inside with damp shoulders and folded umbrellas. The rubber mat by the door grows darker by degrees. Water beads on the edge of the counter where someone sets down an umbrella without thinking. Each time the door opens, the air changes for a second. Wet wool. Cold concrete. Traffic washed cleaner than usual.

People come in shaking umbrellas, water droplets darkening the mat.

A parent buys children's paracetamol with the frantic calm of someone trying not to panic. The bottle lands on the counter a little too hard. The parent apologises for nothing. Sober scans it, asks the child's age, repeats the dosage once, then once again slower. The parent nods too quickly, pays, and leaves with the bottle held like a tool rather than a product.

A teenager asks about acne products without meeting her eyes. His hood is damp around the edges. He keeps one hand in his pocket and pretends to study ingredients he does not understand. Sober does not crowd him. She steps beside the shelf, not too near, and taps one box lightly with her finger.

"That one's a good place to start."

He glances at it, then at her, then back to the shelf. "Thanks."

A man in a suit buys breath mints and looks at his watch twice in the same minute.

He smells faintly of rain and printer toner. His tie is slightly off-centre. He taps his card before she has finished naming the amount, then apologises with the distracted embarrassment of someone already late for the next thing.

"It's one of those days," he says.

Sober hands over the mints. "Seems popular."

He gives a short laugh that isn't really about humour and goes.

The door chime rings and rings.

A woman asks where the batteries are and then says she didn't realise pharmacies sold them.

An elderly man wants to know whether this cough syrup is the same as the old cough syrup, because the box looks different and he does not trust packaging changes. Sober reads the fine print with him, line by line, and shows him where the active ingredient sits in small black lettering. He nods only when the chemistry agrees with his memory.

Two schoolgirls come in for lip balm and leave with lip balm and tissues and a packet of gum they did not plan to buy.

A courier arrives with stock in two cardboard boxes strapped with plastic tape. He leaves rain footprints across the lino and says, "Sorry," without slowing down. Sober signs the pad, cuts the tape with the small blade she keeps in the drawer, and stacks the unopened boxes against the wall for later. Maya will sort them when the afternoon shift starts.

She moves between the shelves, steady. Her warmth is small and real. She does not overreach.

That is part of why people come back.

She does not perform concern. She offers enough of it to be useful.

At the consult corner a woman in activewear asks whether magnesium really helps with sleep or whether that is something the internet decided this month. A young tradie with plaster dust still at the seam of his sleeves wants pain relief strong enough to get him through the afternoon but not strong enough to make him stupid on the ladder tomorrow. Sober answers both in the same tone. Calm. Practical. Not cold.

By one o'clock, the rain has thinned to a damp brightness outside the shopfront.

Cars move past with water still clinging low to their tyres. Across the street, someone from the bakery wipes metal chairs with a grey cloth and gives up halfway through when another burst of drizzle starts. A bus kneels at the curb and rises again. Pedestrians hunch and un-hunch depending on what the sky is doing.

Sober writes up a script, staples a receipt, slides a box across the counter, wipes her hands on the sides of her apron, and glances once at the clock.

Not because she is waiting for anything.

Just because routine moves best when marked.

In the early afternoon, a stranger arrives with a folder tucked under his arm.

His shoes are too clean for the weather. His trousers have that pressed look of a day spent indoors. The folder is not wet. He has either parked close or cares enough about paper to have protected it with his own body. His smile is calibrated.

"Ms.," he says, glancing at the name badge she never wears but that he has somehow learned anyway. "Thanks for making time."

His voice is smooth in the way voices get when they are used professionally. Not oily exactly. Just too ready.

Sober looks at him once, then at the folder, then back to the customer she is handing change to.

"I didn't," she says, but not unkindly.

The customer, a regular who buys the same antihistamines every fortnight and always folds the receipt into exact quarters before putting it in his wallet, looks between them with mild interest and then thinks better of it.

Sober gestures toward the back room. "You can talk. Five minutes."

The man smiles as if this is close enough to a win.

He follows her past the staff-only sign as if it doesn't apply to him.

In the back room, boxes are stacked neatly. A small fridge hums. A ledger sits open where she left it.

There is a narrow sink with one mug beside it, clean but not put away. A tea towel hangs from the handle of a low cupboard. The fluorescent light back here is colder than out front. No display shelving. No soft customer voice. Just stock, storage, invoices, and the practical spine of the shop.

Sober does not sit.

The representative notices and remains standing too, though only after a small pause in which he had clearly expected a more conversational arrangement.

He opens the folder on the table and slides papers forward with the confidence of someone who has done this a hundred times.

The paper is thick. The print is clean. Colour logo in the top corner. Headings bolded. There is even a glossy mock-up of a possible refit tucked inside the sleeve: brighter shelving, more neutral branding, less character pretending to be more modern.

"Acquisition," he says. "A partnership. We keep the neighbourhood feel. We keep your name on the sign, if you want. We take the admin off your hands. You get stability."

The word stability lands with weight.

The fridge hums beneath it.

Somewhere out front, the door chime rings and then is muffled by the wall. Someone speaks. A customer laugh, brief and ordinary. The world continues while a man in clean shoes tries to buy part of her life.

The last year has been full of costs that no one sees.

Rent.

Stock.

Electricity.

Insurance.

The small leak in the ceiling she paid to have fixed before it became a bigger leak.

The printer that jams only when she is busiest.

The quiet exhaustion of being responsible for everything every day.

The responsibility is not poetic. It is bins and invoices and remembering when the anti-nausea scripts are due from the wholesaler and noticing when the till paper is nearly out before it actually runs out. It is not forgetting to turn the closed sign around. It is carrying cartons in the morning and smiling at strangers five minutes later.

Sober looks at the papers without touching them.

"Why?" she asks.

He laughs softly.

Not rude. Not quite patronising. Just the laugh of someone who assumes the answer is flattering.

"Because you're doing well. This is a good location. Good customer base. You've built trust."

Trust.

A word that has been broken and repaired in her mouth until it no longer feels abstract.

She thinks of the regular customer who leans on the counter and asks about her day.

He does not really want the full answer, and that is fine. What he offers is not intimacy. It is repetition. Recognition. The shape of being known in public without being claimed.

She thinks of the teenager who came back last week and quietly said thank you.

Not for magic. Not for being saved. Just for not making him ask twice.

She thinks of the way people pronounce her name like it matters that someone knows it.

The representative keeps talking, filling the silence as if silence is a gap to be closed.

"We can upgrade the fit-out. New signage. Better stock flow. You can take weekends off. You can breathe."

He says breathe like he is handing her permission.

Sober's fingers curl into a fist at her side, not because she is angry at him, but because part of her wants it.

Part of her wants an easier shape to live inside.

A version of the shop where someone else chases invoices. Someone else handles rostering. Someone else absorbs late deliveries, ordering errors, rent negotiations, broken lights, and all the other small frictions that take bites out of a day before the day has properly started.

She can picture it too easily.

A cleaner back room.

A newer fridge.

A better till system.

Corporate discounts on stock.

Time off that is real instead of theoretical.

The temptation is not greed. It is relief.

That is what makes it dangerous.

The representative mistakes her silence for opening.

He places one finger lightly on the top page and taps a figure halfway down.

"We'd make it worth your while."

Sober looks not at the number but at his hand.

Dry cuff. Short clean nail. Wedding ring. A hand that probably hands over pens more often than it lifts boxes.

Then she thinks of another part of her, the part that left without running.

The part that built this shop out of routine and choice.

The part that learned that comfort can be a trap if it comes at the cost of your own centre.

She remembers signing the lease in a too-bright office with a real estate agent who kept saying things like boutique potential and up-and-coming strip. She remembers painting one wall herself because the quote for painters was stupid and the old colour annoyed her. She remembers the first week with half-empty shelves and too much echo. She remembers the first regular who came back. The first month she broke even. The first time someone asked, "Are you the owner?" and said, "It's nice in here," with surprise rather than politeness.

None of that felt grand.

It felt earned.

She looks at him and sees, for a brief second, how he has mistaken her tiredness for weakness.

"I'm not selling," she says.

He blinks.

"You haven't seen the number."

"I'm not selling," she repeats, and the repetition feels like laying a brick. "I'm tired. That doesn't mean I'm for sale."

The room holds still for a moment after that.

Only the fridge hum. Only the distant murmur of shop noise through the wall. Only rain ticking lightly somewhere outside against metal.

His smile falters, then resets.

The reset is quick enough that, if she did not spend half her life reading faces, she might miss it.

"We can revisit. Sometimes people need time."

Sober nods once, as if to say: you can leave now.

He gathers the papers, but not all of them. One glossy sheet remains half out of the folder for a second before he notices and slides it back in. The choreography of professional retreat. No argument. No pressure that could be named pressure. Just the soft persistence of people who assume access is a matter of timing.

At the door he gives her one more version of the smile.

"We admire what you've built."

This time she says nothing.

He leaves through the back room, and she follows only far enough to make sure he actually goes.

Out front, the door chime rings as he exits. One of the customers near the vitamins glances over at him and then back to a label. The world refuses to stage his departure.

When he is gone, she sits in the back room alone and listens to the fridge hum.

The sound is small and steady.

It makes the room feel real.

She notices the chair before she sits in it. Aluminium legs. Vinyl seat with one small crack near the back edge. She lowers herself carefully anyway, elbows on knees, eyes on the floor tiles. One tile is a slightly different shade from the others where something was replaced years ago. Near the sink there is a dark crescent of water from where she rinsed a mug earlier and forgot to wipe under it.

She does not feel triumphant.

She feels clear.

Not light. Not vindicated. Not newly transformed by refusing a thing.

Just aligned.

The difference matters.

She sits there long enough for her breathing to slow all the way back down. Long enough to hear a customer cough out front. Long enough for the rhythm of the shop to return to being the larger fact.

Then she stands, straightens the papers he left behind without looking at them, and drops them into the recycling bin.

Not violently.

Just decisively.

The papers slide down against flattened cardboard and old stock invoices with a soft dry sound.

She washes her hands though she hasn't touched anything dirty.

Soap. Water. Paper towel.

The motions are ordinary enough to let the rest of her catch up.

Out front, the door chime rings.

Another customer.

Another need.

Sober steps back onto the shop floor, pulls on her practiced smile, and lets it be real because she chooses it.

A woman with damp hair wants antihistamines and tissues.

A man in a council polo asks whether she stocks blister pads for steel-capped boots.

Two tourists with umbrellas dripping onto the mat want directions to the nearest urgent care because their hotel receptionist told them pharmacies know everything.

Sober answers. Points. Reaches. Scans. Bags.

One of the tourists says, "Sorry, you're probably busy."

Sober hands over the directions she has written on the back of a duplicate receipt.

"It's alright."

And it is.

Not because the day is easy.

Because usefulness steadies her.

Later, in the lull between customers, she notices the landline phone on the counter and feels a sharp memory of last night's ring.

The phone is where it always is.

Cream plastic. Curled cord. Slight yellowing near the base. It looks almost stubborn in daylight, as if refusing to become quaint. A practical object with a long memory.

She does not touch it.

Her hands go to the work she can do.

Restocking.

Counting.

Checking expiry dates.

She lifts a box, turns it, reads the date, returns it to the shelf front-facing. Her fingers know the movement better than thought. Another box. Another. The rhythm is not enough to erase memory, but it gives memory somewhere to sit without taking over the room.

A city's small needs keep moving.

She keeps moving with them.

A regular comes in for blood pressure tablets and tells her his daughter passed her driving test on the third go.

"Third time lucky," he says.

Sober smiles. "Still counts."

He laughs. "That's what I told her."

A woman buys expensive hand cream and asks if the rain is supposed to keep up all week, as though pharmacists also manage the weather. Sober says, "Feels like it," and the woman nods as if that settles something.

A child drags sticky fingers across the lower shelf of vitamins while his mother compares brands.

Sober gets a cloth and wipes the fingerprints off later.

The rain stops properly by late afternoon.

Outside the shopfront, the footpath begins to steam in patches where weak sun reaches through. Umbrellas disappear one by one. People move faster now that the sky has made up its mind.

Inside, the shop smells less of wet coats and more of hand cream again.

The day closes around its own shape.

Not spectacular.

Not saved.

Held.

And somewhere beneath all of it, where she keeps the things she does not name often, there is a quiet recognition that this, too, is character: not only what breaks you, but what you keep choosing after.

Chapter Six: Apothecary

The wellness clinic is everything the chain pharmacy isn't.

Warm light. Wood shelves. Chalkboard signs in looping handwriting. Glass jars of herbs lined up like old magic. The air smells of citrus and something vaguely medicinal, like a promise.

The front window is dressed with folded linen, pale ceramics, bunches of dried lavender tied with twine. A small brass bell sits near the register though no one seems to use it. Everything in the shop suggests slowness on purpose. Nothing fluorescent. Nothing plastic unless it has been hidden well.

Drink stands at the entrance with the cat carrier on the floor beside him.

The door closes softly behind him. Not a chime. Just a cushioned click.

People drift past in linen shirts and clean sneakers. Their faces are calm in a way that feels rehearsed. A woman with expensive glasses holds two amber bottles up to the light as if choosing wine. A man in running gear studies a display called Mineral Support with the concentration of someone trying to optimise being alive. Near the back, someone laughs softly at something that cannot matter much.

The floorboards do not creak. Even that feels curated.

A woman behind the counter smiles at him as if he is already welcome.

"First time?"

He nods.

"Beautiful," she says, gesturing around as if she's showing him a garden. "Take your time. Let your body tell you what it needs."

"I'm looking for someone," Drink says.

The pharmacist waits.

"Laurel. She's a pharmacist."

The pharmacist glances toward the dispensary, then back to him.

"Not here."

No apology. No elaboration. Just the fact, set down neatly.

Drink nods once and steps aside so a woman with a yoga mat strapped across her back can reach the counter. The woman smells faintly of rain and eucalyptus. She asks whether the mushroom powder is the same one as last month or whether they changed the supplier again because the last one was more grounding. The pharmacist answers in a low, even voice. Adaptogenic blend. Better sourcing. Slightly different finish.

Drink stands there one second too long before remembering to move.

His body needs a drink. His body is a liar.

He walks the aisles slowly, reading labels with words that seem designed to slip around accountability.

Detox.

Cleanse.

Reset.

Renewal.

Start again.

The words are printed in soft colours on matte cardboard. Sage green. Cream. Clay pink. Fonts chosen to feel trustworthy. Nothing in the room raises its voice. Even the sales language pretends not to be selling.

A shelf of teas promises Sleep Support and Hormone Balance and Digestive Ease. Another offers drops for focus, calm, immunity, mood. A chalkboard sign near the back says *Daily rituals shape the life you return to*. The handwriting is careful enough to look effortless.

Drink stops at a display of tonics in amber glass.

One promises clarity.

Another promises sleep.

Another promises confidence.

The bottles sit in neat rows on a reclaimed timber crate as if order itself might heal you.

Beside him, two women in activewear speak in low voices while comparing labels.

"This one has ashwagandha," one says.

"Does it work?"

She shrugs. "It tastes like dirt, so hopefully."

They laugh softly and move on.

Drink picks up one of the bottles and turns it over.

Ingredients. Suggested use. Shake well.

The glass is cool in his hand.

He puts it back exactly where it was.

On the far wall there is a mirror framed in pale wood. Someone has written above it in neat script: *You are becoming.*

Drink stops in front of it.

His reflection looks thinner than he expects. His eyes are tired. The beard he has not properly trimmed makes his face look more uncertain around the edges. His shirt is clean enough but wrinkled from the carrier strap. He looks like a man performing being okay.

The mirror does not change anything. It only repeats him.

A woman passes behind him carrying a basket of rolled hand towels and small white sample cups. In the reflection, for half a second, it looks like she is part of the same display as the jars and signs and polished timber. The whole place is selling a life before it sells a product.

Drink looks away first.

Near the dispensary hatch, a small stack of appointment cards sits under a sign that reads *Holistic consultations available. Bookings essential.* A man in a cream sweater is asking about gut health with the solemnity of a confession. The staff member nods as if his intestine is a character in a story she has heard before.

Drink moves deeper into the shop.

The cat shifts inside the carrier at his ankle, steadying himself with a quiet rustle of fabric. Drink glances down. Through the mesh, two eyes watch the moving feet of strangers with measured distrust. The cat does not complain. He just keeps adjusting to the world as it bumps him.

A clerk approaches with a small basket of samples.

She is younger than the pharmacist, hair tied back with a ribbon that looks accidental and probably isn't. Her smile is soft in the way the room asks for.

"We've got a new herbal blend for cravings," she says, voice low, conspiratorial. "It helps take the edge off."

The phrase take the edge off hits him like a hand around his throat.

The room stays warm. The shelves stay neat. Somewhere near the front counter someone asks if the magnesium spray can go in hand luggage. A jar lid clicks shut. The world continues politely.

Drink hears only the phrase.

Take the edge off.

He imagines the pub's warm light.

He imagines the bottle in the bin.

He imagines the first swallow and the immediate silence afterward.

He can almost feel the soft collapse that used to come with it. The world narrowing into something manageable. The debt arriving later.

He forces a smile.

"Thanks."

She drops a small sachet into his hand.

It is light as paper. He can feel nothing through it. Still, he holds it like it matters.

The sachet says *Craving Ease* in muted lettering over a drawing of leaves. On the back: *steep for four minutes. Best enjoyed mindfully.*

He closes his fingers around it until the paper bends.

A man nearby talks loudly about his morning routine.

"Ice bath," he says, as if he's listing moral achievements. "Meditation. No sugar. No alcohol. It's about discipline."

He stands near the collagen powders wearing a fitted black shirt and a watch that could cover someone's rent for a week. The woman with him nods in that patient way people do when they are either impressed or trapped.

"I just think," he continues, "people make it too complicated. Your body tells you what it needs if you're willing to listen."

Drink hears himself in the man's voice and hates it.

Not because the words are wrong exactly. Because he knows what it is to speak like that when control is still mostly theatre.

He moves away before he has to hear the rest.

The carrier bumps against his leg. The cat shifts inside, unimpressed.

Drink finds a shelf with plain supplements.

B vitamins.

Magnesium.

Electrolytes.

Things in white tubs and pharmacy-style boxes. Less story. Less aspiration. Things that don't pretend to be salvation.

He takes them because he wants something real.

A woman beside him reaches for probiotic capsules and says, mostly to herself, "I miss when things were just vitamins."

Drink glances at her. Late forties maybe. Grocery tote over one shoulder. Wet umbrella tucked badly under one arm.

She notices him looking and half smiles.

"No offence," she says, nodding toward the nearest chalkboard sign. "I just came in for zinc."

Drink almost smiles back.

"Yeah."

She takes her box and leaves him there.

That tiny exchange settles him more than the sachet in his hand.

At the end of the aisle there is a low table set with tiny cups of something amber.

A handwritten card reads *Complimentary seasonal tonic.* A staff member invites a couple to try some. They do, politely. One of them says, "Oh, that's earthy," in the tone people use when they mean not good but still expensive enough to respect.

Drink keeps walking.

Near the counter a woman with a pram asks whether they stock children's probiotics safe for toddlers with eczema. A different staff member crouches to show her options from the lower shelf. Not rushed. Not cold. The child in the pram sucks two fingers and stares at the ceiling lights.

For a second Drink thinks of the kind of shop Sober would run.

Not in sentiment. In contrast.

Her place would have fluorescent lights and practical labels and nothing in jars unless it has to be. People would ask direct questions and get direct answers. Dosage. Timing. Side effects. No one there would tell a customer to listen to their inner self and see what aligns.

He can picture her behind the counter with exact clarity.

Hair tied in a braid.

Hands moving without hurry.

Small kindnesses measured to be useful.

The memory lands hard enough that he has to look down at the carrier and count to five before moving again.

At the counter, the clerk wraps his purchases carefully.

Paper folded neat. A small sticker pressed flat over the seam. The bag handles turned inward so it looks less like a bag and more like a gift.

As if ritual can fix what it touches.

The clerk scans the sachet too, then pauses.

"Oh," she says. "That one's complimentary."

Drink nods.

The register screen glows softly. The numbers look too clean to belong to him.

He taps his card.

Approved.

The machine chirps once.

"Proud of you," she says lightly, not knowing the weight of those words.

It is probably about choosing supplements. Or choosing health. Or buying things from a shop that sells improvement in amber bottles.

Drink nods because correcting her would take too much energy.

He swallows.

"Sorry. One more thing. Laurel. She's a pharmacist. You wouldn't happen to know her?"

The clerk tilts her head, thinking.

Then she shakes it once.

"No, sorry. I don't know that name."

He says, "Alright."

She slides the paper bag toward him. "Take care."

He picks up the carrier and leaves before the phrase can mean anything.

Outside, the air is cooler.

The City's noises return all at once. A bus groans at the curb. A dog barks from somewhere up the block. Someone swears at a taxi that has stopped too far from the rank. Tyres hiss over damp road. A construction sign rattles slightly in the wind.

The apothecary door closes behind him with the same soft click as before. Its warm window remains intact, serene, already forgetting him.

Drink walks to a bench and gently lowers the cat carrier before sitting.

The bench is metal, still slightly wet and colder than it looks. The paper bag rests on his lap. Through the shop window he can still see the mirror on the far wall if he angles his head right. He looks away.

A couple walks past sharing a takeaway salad and discussing a Pilates instructor named Nina who apparently changed their posture and their life. A cyclist rings a bell and slips between pedestrians. A man in office clothes stands under an awning eating a muffin directly over the wrapper with the concentration of someone who cannot spare a crumb on his tie.

Drink pulls out his phone and opens the notes app again.

The earlier line waits for him.

City. Three pharmacies.

Below it, the first tick.

Below that, the second.

He types a new line:

Worthy is a trap.

The words look strange on the screen.

Too polished. Too self-aware. Like something copied from a meeting handout or a fridge magnet or the inside of someone else's notebook.

He deletes them.

He types instead:

Show up. Do not demand.

That sits better.

Still blunt. Still a little childish. But true enough to keep.

He stares at the earlier line.

City. Three pharmacies.

The shape of the plan had looked almost solid this morning. Now it looks small and embarrassing. A scavenger hunt powered by shame.

He imagines Sober behind a counter, hands moving without hurry, voice warm in small doses.

He imagines her sleep broken by the landline ring.

Shame rises like heat, quick and suffocating.

He locks the phone and puts it away.

Beside him, the cat shifts and presses once against the side mesh as if testing the world through fabric. Drink puts his hand against the carrier. The cat leans his head into the pressure for a second, then settles again.

The contact is small.

It is enough to keep Drink from floating away.

A man waiting for the lights to change glances at the carrier and says, "That yours?"

Drink nods.

"Doesn't look thrilled."

"No."

The man smiles once, brief and tired. "Fair enough."

Then the pedestrian light changes and he goes.

Drink sits there another minute.

Across the street, a florist sweeps wet leaves toward the gutter. A woman in scrubs eats chips from a paper bag while checking her phone. Somewhere above street level, an alarm starts beeping from a truck in reverse and keeps beeping long after anyone could possibly need the warning.

He stands.

He follows the plan because following the plan is the only thing that makes the hours pass without collapse.

At the station, the bin is still there.

The mini bottle is gone.

Someone else took it or the cleaner threw it away. The City resolves choices without ceremony.

Drink stops looking at the bin and keeps moving.

The station smells like wet concrete, brake dust, and burnt coffee from the kiosk near the barriers. People queue in loose lines that aren't quite lines. A student with headphones bigger than his face leans against a pillar tapping one foot. A woman in business clothes talks too loudly into her phone about a delayed settlement. A cleaner pushes a yellow mop bucket past all of them and nobody really sees him.

Drink taps on through the gate.

The carrier handle digs into his palm. He switches hands.

On the platform, a man in work boots sleeps sitting up, chin down on his chest, lunch esky between his feet. Two teenagers share chips and insult each other with ritual affection. An older woman unwraps a lozenge with slow, furious care. The loudspeaker announces delays in a voice too calm to be useful.

Drink sits on the edge of a bench and counts stops on the digital board as if counting could shorten distance.

Somewhere between stations, a text from his sponsor arrives.

Talk tomorrow?

The message is plain. No lecture. No pressure. Just the next fact.

Drink stares at it.

His first impulse is to avoid. To disappear. To let silence answer for him. To make absence do the talking because absence is easier to maintain than honesty.

He types one word and sends it before he can change his mind.

Yeah.

The reply does not come immediately, which is its own kind of respect.

A train rushes through the opposite platform without stopping, wind snapping at coats and loose paper. The cat crouches lower in the carrier, ears angled back. Drink lowers one hand to the mesh until the train has gone.

When his own train arrives, the doors slide open with a sigh.

He boards with everyone else.

The carriage is half full. A child kicks the back of a seat three rows away while his mother apologises to no one in particular. A man in a collared shirt scrolls job listings. A woman eats sushi from a supermarket tray with wooden chopsticks and looks out the window without seeing much.

Drink sits and sets the carrier on the seat beside him until more people get on at the next stop and he moves it back to his lap.

The cat's weight is slight but constant.

Drink holds the carrier handle loosely, as if he's learning how to hold things without crushing them.

Outside, streets slide past.

Shopfronts.

Back fences.

Laundry on balconies.

A mural half-finished on a brick wall.

A bottle shop sign flashing red against the early dark.

He looks at it once and then at his own knees.

The train keeps moving.

The City keeps moving.

He sits through the discomfort.

He counts stops like breaths.

When the carriage lights reflect back at him in the darkened window, his face floats over the passing suburbs for a second and then breaks apart again.

He does not feel enlightened.

He does not feel stronger.

He feels scraped out, tired, and still in motion.

For now, that will have to do.

Chapter Seven: The Child

In the late afternoon, the shop fills with a different kind of noise.

Not louder, exactly. Thinner. Sharper around the edges. The after-school hour. Parents stopping in on the way home. Children tired enough to cry over the wrong thing. Office workers picking up one last item before the train. The door chime sounds more often. The air shifts each time it opens. Damp jackets. Supermarket bags. Traffic cooled by evening. The floor near the entrance gathers the day's small grit from shoes and wheels and weather.

The fluorescent strips overhead continue to hum faintly.

At the counter, someone asks for bandages and a pregnancy test in the same breath and then blushes as if the items belong to separate worlds. A man in paint-splattered work pants wants something for his feet and keeps checking his phone while she scans them. A child near the generic glasses rack rolls a drink bottle with one foot until it bumps the display and falls over with a hollow plastic clatter.

Sober picks it up and sets it upright.

The child says, "Sorry."

"It's alright," she says.

The mother gives a tired nod without really looking up from the shelf of cough medicine.

Outside the front window, the sky is flattening toward evening.

Cars move past in slow, regular bands. Headlights catch on the glass and slide away. Across the street, two children kick a ball against a low wall while a parent talks into a phone with one hand over the pram handle. Somewhere farther down the strip, a dog barks once and is answered by another.

A parent comes in carrying a child who is too quiet.

That is what changes the room.

Not panic. Not drama. Just the wrong kind of stillness.

The child's head rests heavy on the parent's shoulder. His cheeks are flushed. His eyes are glossy, unfocused.

The parent is moving too fast for steadiness and too slowly for calm. One hand keeps readjusting the child's weight though there is no better way to hold him. The bag on their shoulder hangs half-open. A packet of wipes sticks out near a bent corner of paperwork.

Sober steps from behind the counter and gestures gently.

"Here," she says, and clears a space at the consult corner, a small area tucked behind a shelf where the light is softer.

She moves a stack of catalogues aside. Straightens the blood pressure chair that no one likes sitting in. Pulls a box of tissues closer without making a point of it. The consult corner is not private, not really, but it is turned slightly away from the main floor, and sometimes that is enough.

The parent lowers into the chair with the care of someone afraid the child will break if set down wrong.

The boy's shoe brushes the edge of the shelf on the way down. One Velcro strap is loose.

The parent's hands shake as they fumble for a wallet. "He's been vomiting since last night," they say, voice tight. "The clinic said… they said to keep him hydrated but he won't—"

Sober listens.

She does not interrupt too early. She does not make the parent repeat things for the sake of sounding thorough. She asks simple questions.

Weight. Age. Last fluids. How long. Immunisation history.

The questions come plain and orderly, each one making the room more manageable by a fraction. The parent answers too fast at first, then slower as the shape of the problem gets spoken aloud.

The child blinks once and turns his face farther into the parent's shoulder.

Sober reaches for the thermometer she keeps in the drawer below the consult counter. The plastic casing is cool and familiar in her hand. She wipes it down from habit before and after, even though there is no time in the moment that truly needs the before.

She does not say it will be fine.

She does not pretend she can fix what is outside her control.

She hands over electrolytes and shows the parent, with a quiet firmness, how to measure. Small sips. Watch the signs. Don't wait too long.

She tears open the box cleanly, folds the insert once, and points with her finger rather than handing over a paragraph of instructions and hoping panic will read it. The sachets rattle softly inside the packet. The parent nods rapidly, then stops and asks her to repeat the measurement again. Sober repeats it exactly the same way.

A man waiting at the scripts counter glances over once, then looks away. A schoolgirl with a backpack nearly as big as she is stands by the fridge of probiotic yoghurts and pretends not to watch. Near the entrance, a toddler begins whining because he wants the snake-shaped lollies from the display bowl and has been told no.

The room keeps happening around the centre of this one small emergency.

The parent's eyes are wet now, but they do not cry. Not properly. There isn't time.

"Thank you," they whisper, like it is the only thing holding them up.

Sober nods back.

"Go now," she says, and her voice is kind because it needs to be. "If he gets worse, go to emergency. Don't second-guess it."

The parent stands too quickly, steadies, shifts the child higher against their shoulder, and gathers the bag, the box, the wallet, the tissues, all the small things that have to come with fear. The child's head lolls once and then settles.

They leave.

The door chime rings and rings, as if echoing the panic that just passed through.

Cold air slips in after them and then is gone.

Sober stands in the consult corner for a moment after they're gone.

She can still feel the warmth of the child in the space they occupied. Not literally. More like an imprint left in the room. The tissue box slightly crooked. The chair still angled out. A smear on the shelf where a damp hand steadied itself.

She feels her own heart beating, steady and alive.

She feels the echo of the child's warm forehead against the parent's shoulder.

Then she turns back to the counter and finds her hands have gone cold.

She rubs them once against each other as if that might be enough. It isn't, but the motion gives her something to do.

At the sink behind the consult corner, she washes her hands. Soap. Water. Paper towel. The water runs lukewarm for a second before it remembers how to be cold. She dries her fingers carefully, folding the paper once before throwing it away. The bin lid knocks shut with a plastic click.

When she steps back onto the floor, the shop accepts her return without ceremony.

A woman asks where the nappy rash cream is.

A man lifts his council polo and says, "Sorry, just quick, do you have something for this?" As he points to a rash.

Sober points. Reaches. Answers.

The bottle-rolling child has moved on to staring at the spinning greeting card rack.

A customer arrives an hour later, rubbing her belly absently.

By then the light outside has shifted again. Less grey. More yellow at the edges. The after-work crowd has started to replace the school crowd. People carry tote bags and train fatigue. Their conversations start halfway through themselves.

The pregnant customer asks about prenatal vitamins and folic acid.

Her smile is bright and nervous. She is excited and afraid in equal measure.

She wears a loose cardigan over exercise clothes, as if the day got away from her before she had a chance to become the right version of herself for it. One shoelace is coming undone. A coffee stain marks the cardboard sleeve of the cup she sets down near the register and then forgets about.

Sober keeps her face calm.

She shows her the right aisle, the right brand, the right dose. She speaks in facts, not feelings.

The customer follows half a step behind, one hand still resting on the slight curve of her stomach as if checking in with it. She picks up one box, then another, then turns both over and stares at the tiny print with the overwhelmed expression of someone discovering there are too many acceptable choices.

Sober takes the boxes gently back and taps the one she means.

"This one."

The woman exhales through a small laugh.

"Sorry," she says. "I'm a bit all over the place."

"It's a lot," Sober says, and the words come out before she can stop them.

Then she adds, carefully, "You're doing the right thing."

The woman's eyes soften.

"Thanks. That helps."

She puts the right box in her basket and keeps one hand on the handle for a second longer than necessary, as if absorbing steadiness by contact.

At the counter, she adds ginger tea, lip balm, and crackers to the purchase as if assembling a kit for a version of herself she has only just met. When Sober names the total, she pats the wrong pocket first, then laughs softly again at herself.

Behind her, a man with a script for blood pressure tablets looks at a wall poster about stroke symptoms while waiting his turn. Two teenagers come in for pimple patches and spend longer choosing the design than the treatment. Someone outside brakes too hard and a horn sounds, brief and irritated.

The pregnant woman pays.

Sober places the vitamins in a paper bag and folds the top once.

The woman takes it with both hands.

"Thanks again."

Sober nods.

When the woman leaves, she pauses outside the shopfront to tuck the bag under her arm and retie her shoelace against the window. Then she straightens and disappears into the flow of the footpath.

Sober watches her walk away and feels something twist in her chest that is not jealousy and not anger.

It is simply the shape of a life she does not have.

Not an accusation. Not even a longing in the cleanest sense. More the outline of an absence, visible because something walked past in roughly the right dimensions.

A child outside squeals as the ball from earlier rolls into the gutter. Someone calls, "Careful." Traffic moves. The automatic doors of the bakery across the street hiss open and shut.

Sober turns back to the till.

She checks the float though it does not need checking. Straightens the counter display of lozenges. Refills the hand sanitiser bottle at the consult desk. Wipes away the ring left by the coffee cup. Routine reclaims the room by small degrees.

Just before closing, a teenager comes in, hood up, hands in pockets.

The sky outside has gone fully evening now. The shop window holds both street reflection and interior light at once. Inside, the fluorescent strips feel harsher after dark. They flatten faces. They make every object look more factual.

The teenager hovers at the acne shelf until Sober steps over and stands near enough to be available, far enough not to trap him.

He is all angles and uncertainty. Too old to be a child in the way adults say the word, too young to have learned how to ask for help cleanly. His school shoes are scuffed at the toes. There is a fading school logo on his hoodie. He pretends to read the back of a cleanser bottle while not absorbing a word.

He clears his throat.

"Do you have… like… something for anxiety?"

Sober's breath catches.

Not visibly, she hopes. The motion happens lower down, somewhere private.

She looks at him, really looks.

His face is young in a way that makes her ache. He is trying to ask for help without learning the language for it.

"There are things that can help," she says gently. "But it depends what you mean. Can you tell me what's happening?"

He shrugs, shoulders up near his ears.

"Just… can't sleep. Heart's going. Mum says I'm being dramatic."

The last word is said without anger. Worse than anger. It lands like something repeated often enough to lose force and gain shape.

Behind them, the fridge unit near the probiotics kicks in with a low mechanical buzz. A customer near the counter asks for a receipt and then changes their mind. The EFTPOS machine chirps approval. From outside comes the faint bass pulse of a car stopped too long at the lights.

Sober keeps her voice level.

"Does it happen at night more?"

He nods.

"Or if you have to go somewhere?"

Another nod. Smaller.

He looks at the shelf while he answers, as if speaking directly to her might make the whole thing less survivable.

"School sometimes."

Sober reaches for a plain box from the sleep support shelf, then stops with her fingers on it.

Not wrong. Just not enough.

She lowers her hand again.

"Some things can help with sleep," she says. "But if your heart's racing a lot, it might be worth seeing a GP too. Just to talk it through properly."

He makes a face like that answer was both expected and inconvenient.

"Yeah."

Sober does not oversell the box she eventually picks up. Chamomile, magnesium, simple ingredients, nothing dramatic. Something to try, not something to believe in.

She explains how to use it. One capsule. Evening. See how you go.

Then she adds, not too softly, "And you're not being dramatic."

The words land between them and stay there.

He looks at her then.

Really looks.

For a second his whole face changes, not into relief exactly, but into the stunned stillness of someone hearing the right sentence too late for it to feel normal.

"Okay," he says.

He takes the box in both hands.

At the counter he pays in coins, counting them twice before sliding them across. His fingers are ink-stained at the side, maybe from class notes, maybe from drawing in the margins of something he was meant to care about. He puts the change straight into his pocket without checking it.

As he turns to leave, he hesitates by the automatic door.

"Thanks."

Sober nods once.

The door opens. Cool air. Street noise. Then he is gone.

Closing takes longer after a day like that, though the tasks are the same.

She locks the scripts drawer. Counts the till. Empties the small bin from the consult corner where tissues and torn cardboard and a crumpled electrolyte insert sit together without meaning to. She returns the chair to its proper angle. Wipes the counter. Checks the fridge log. Turns one sign around, then another.

Each action lands back inside the familiar groove of evening.

Outside, children are still in the small park down the road, using the last of the light badly. Someone calls out for a scooter to be brought in. A football thuds once against metal railing. A baby cries somewhere beyond sight, then stops as quickly as it started.

Sober kills the front aisle lights one row at a time.

The shop narrows.

Warmth leaves the corners first.

In the dimmer after-light, the consult corner looks smaller than it did during the day. Just a chair. A shelf. A box of tissues. Nothing dramatic about it. Nothing sacred. A place where people briefly bring the bodies and worries they can't carry neatly in public.

She stands there for one second longer than she needs to.

Then she turns away.

At the door, she flips the sign to CLOSED.

Her reflection catches faintly in the glass over the word. Tired face. Hair escaping slightly at the temples. Apron creased. A woman who held the line all day and is now allowed to feel the weight of having done it.

Not collapse.

Just weight.

She checks the lock with her hand.

The metal is cool.

The street outside is already moving on to night.

Chapter Eight: Hospital

The hospital is a place that doesn't pretend.

It doesn't sell comfort as wellness. It doesn't hide panic behind pastel packaging. It doesn't say reset or cleanse or become.

It says triage.

Drink walks through the automatic doors with the cat carrier in one hand and his phone in the other, the screen lit with nothing useful. Outside, the City is noise and motion and appetite. Inside, everything is sharper. Clean, cold air. The bite of antiseptic. A sweetness underneath it that isn't sweet at all.

Bodies. Fear. Time.

For a moment the rhythm of people being called through the doors folds into another memory.

A small registry office.

Laurel beside him in a dress she had chosen because it was simple and didn't make a ceremony out of something they already knew.

Two witnesses. A bored clerk. A pen scratching loudly on paper.

He had fumbled the signature line and Laurel had leaned in just enough to murmur, "Easy, Linc."

Outside the building someone on the steps had been singing a playground rhyme while they waited for the door to open again.

Drink remembers catching only one line before it was swallowed by the street.

Then comes marriage.

He snaps back to the present and slows, because his body wants to turn this into a threshold. Wants to make it a doorway he can fail at.

The automatic doors close behind him with a sigh.

For a second the outside noise thins to glass-muted traffic and the broad mechanical life of the building takes over. Air vents. Rubber soles on polished floor. A distant trolley rattling over a join in the lino. Somewhere deeper in the hospital, an alarm sounds once and then stops, not urgent enough to be panic, too common to matter to anyone who works here.

A security guard's eyes follow him, not cruelly, just the way you watch someone who looks like they might fall over.

The guard stands near a pillar under a TV that no one is really watching. Middle-aged, tired, utility vest over dark clothes, radio clipped near his shoulder. The television above him runs a daytime program with the volume low and the captions on. A smiling host says something about heart health while three people in the waiting area stare past it.

"Pets aren't allowed," the guard says, already tired of saying it.

Drink opens his mouth. Almost argues. Almost does the old thing where he tries to make the world bend because he feels desperate.

Instead, he nods once.

"Yeah. Sorry."

There's a reception desk off to the side. A woman behind it glances up, sees the carrier, and makes a small face that says she has rules but also a heart she can't turn off entirely.

She is working between two screens and a stack of clipboards. Her lanyard is twisted. A paper cup sits near her elbow with lipstick on the lid. Behind her, laminated signs crowd a pinboard. *Visiting hours. Lost property. Zero tolerance for aggression. Interpreter services available.* A poster reminding people to wash their hands.

"We can hold it," she says, as if she's talking about a bag of groceries. "For a little while. You'll have to sign."

Drink hesitates with the pen in his hand. The cat shifts in the carrier. A soft scrape. A quiet thump. Present. Alive. Not impressed.

The reception counter smells faintly of disinfectant wipes and warm printer plastic. A cheap plastic chain tethers the pen to a square base. The sign-in sheet is already full of other names and worse handwriting. He writes his details too carefully, as if legibility might make him look less out of place.

"I'll be quick," Drink says, as if quick is something you can promise in a place like this.

The receptionist takes the carrier and slides it behind the desk where it won't be stepped on. The cat's eyes watch Drink through the mesh as if to say: *Don't make this dramatic. Just come back.*

Drink's hand lingers on the handle for a second too long, then he lets go.

He walks deeper into the hospital.

The waiting area is a low-lit aquarium of people holding themselves together.

Metal-framed chairs are arranged in rows that encourage patience without ever producing it. A vending machine hums against one wall, all soft drinks and fluorescent chips, its coin slot taped over with a printed sign that says CARD ONLY. Beside it sits a water fountain with a paper cup dispenser half empty. A child-sized mural of sea creatures covers one section of wall near a play corner nobody is using.

A man rocks in his chair, the motion small but relentless. A woman stares at the wall as if there's a door in it only she can see. A child cries and is shushed softly, the parent's voice frayed into thread.

Near the triage desk, a tired nurse calls a surname that no one answers to the first time. She calls it again, louder, with the flat patience of someone who has already had too many variations of this day. A teenager in a school jacket limps past with an ice pack against one shin. An older woman peels back the edge of a hospital band and checks it for no reason that matters.

Drink feels the pressure rise behind his ribs. The old solution flashes bright and simple.

Leave. Find warmth. Find a pub. Find a bottle.

His mouth goes dry.

He doesn't move.

Standing still at thresholds makes the pressure climb. He remembers that. He starts walking, slow and deliberate, like he's moving through water and the water wants him to stop.

The pharmacy window is set behind glass, fluorescent and clinical. A tired pharmacist speaks to a patient with a voice that has repeated the same instructions too many times. Their eyes are kind, but exhausted. Kindness here is a limited resource.

Drink joins the line.

There are only three people in front of him, but the line has hospital time in it. It does not measure itself in numbers. It measures itself in pauses. In verification. In someone needing the dosage repeated. In someone fumbling Medicare cards out of the wrong section of a wallet. In staff disappearing through a back door and not reappearing quickly enough to satisfy anyone standing still.

In front of him, a woman clutches a plastic bag of medications to her chest as if it's a life raft. Her hands tremble. The label reads a name Drink doesn't know. The tremor is in the woman, not the paper.

Ahead of her, an injured worker in hi-vis shifts his weight off one foot and winces each time he forgets and puts it back. Dried plaster dust clings to the seam of his trouser leg. He keeps checking the same message thread on his phone, thumb hovering over the keyboard without typing. A little further off, an elderly couple sit side by side sharing one folded pamphlet about discharge instructions. The husband is reading it aloud in a low stubborn voice. The wife keeps stopping him to ask what line he's on.

No one is angry. No one is dramatic. Everyone is simply trying not to fall apart in public.

The line moves.

Drink's heartbeat does not.

He watches the staff behind the pharmacy window. A pharmacist prints labels. Another checks a tray. A tech wheels out a grey plastic crate of boxed meds and signs something on a clipboard. A phone rings behind the glass and no one gets to it for four full rings because everyone is already busy with the thing in front of them.

When it's his turn, he steps forward and says the name like he's pushing it through his teeth.

"Laurel."

The pharmacist pauses for a fraction too long.

Drink feels that pause like a hand on his throat.

"She's a pharmacist," he adds quickly, as if that makes him less strange. "I thought she might work here."

The pharmacist is younger than he expected and older than he hoped. Mid-thirties maybe. Hair pinned back badly at the end of a long shift. Their lanyard has twisted so the ID faces inward. There is a red mark on the bridge of their nose from glasses worn too long. They look at Drink with the professional neutrality of someone deciding whether this is going to become difficult.

"Not here," they say.

Drink nods, but doesn't step away.

It would be easier if the answer had force in it. A clear stop. But the answer is just a fact, and facts leave room for more wanting.

"I'm sorry," he says, because suddenly that seems like the thing he is actually saying, though to whom he isn't sure.

The pharmacist waits.

Behind him, someone in the queue exhales loudly. Not hostile. Just tired.

Drink shifts aside half a step, enough to be less in the way, not enough to leave.

A nurse wheels a portable machine past the end of the pharmacy corridor, the wheels clicking over the tiles. Somewhere in the waiting room a baby starts crying again, high and furious now. The security guard glances over, then away.

"That's all I know," the pharmacist says, already turning slightly toward the next script basket.

Drink nods again. "Right."

He steps away from the counter, but not far.

There is a row of chairs opposite the pharmacy window. He sits in the end one because it gives him a view of both the counter and the corridor and because sitting feels less like failing than leaving. The metal seat is colder than the room. A laminated armrest divides him from the empty chair beside him. He places both hands flat on his thighs to keep them useful.

This is the boss here, he thinks without using those words.

Not the pharmacist.

Not the building.

It is waiting.

It is the refusal of the world to hurry for your discomfort.

A nurse calls a name. A couple stands. A child stops crying. Someone laughs softly, unexpectedly, and the sound feels wrong in this place, like sunlight through dirty glass.

Drink watches the pharmacy window again.

Staff go in and out through a doorway behind the counter. A staff-only gap. A hidden world where people carry controlled substances and small bags and hard truths.

He thinks: She would have walked through a doorway like that once. She would have worn a lanyard. She would have known the codes. She would have belonged.

He swallows.

Time in the waiting area loosens around the edges.

A cleaner pushes a yellow mop bucket through the corridor and parks it under a sign no one reads. A vending machine selection fails for a teenage boy in a school jumper and he hits the return button three times before giving up and buying water instead. The injured worker in hi-vis finally sits down and takes his boot off one eyelet at a time, jaw set hard against the effort. The elderly couple finish the pamphlet and begin reading it again from the top as if repetition might improve its manners.

Drink's mouth tastes stale and wrong.

He thinks about the bar outside the hospital he passed on the corner. Warm light. Open door. Someone laughing into the weather. He can feel the path to it in his body like a remembered staircase.

He stays where he is.

The television above the guard changes programs. The captions flicker to a newsreader talking over footage of traffic and politicians and weather maps. None of it seems possible from here. The hospital has its own weather. Recycled cool air. Human heat. Fluorescent fatigue.

A woman near him unwraps a muesli bar and the smell of oats and chocolate suddenly makes him nauseous.

He looks down at his hands instead.

Dry hands. No shake.

That means nothing and also something.

A man nearby, older, in a hospital gown, talks to his daughter on speakerphone. His voice is loud in the way sick people become loud, as if volume might keep them here.

"I told you," The man says, "I'm not going to that chain one anymore. I like the little chemist. The one with the warm light. She actually listens."

His daughter's voice crackles tinny through the speaker. "Dad, you can't just—"

"I can," he says. "That place on Harrow Street. You know the one. Around the park. The lady with the braid. The independent one."

The words cut through Drink like a blade.

Harrow Street. Around the park.

The woman with the braid.

Warm light.

A little chemist.

Drink sits very still, like any movement might make the information evaporate.

The man keeps talking, complaining about parking, about the City, about nurses who "never give you a straight answer." The daughter hushes him and he huffs. The phone speaker crackles. A nurse passes without reacting. Nothing in the room marks the moment except Drink's pulse stumbling in his throat.

He stands up slowly.

Not in a rush. Rushing is how he used to run.

He walks back to the counter and waits until the pharmacist looks up again.

"Sorry," Drink says. His voice sounds foreign in his own mouth. "I'm not trying to put you in a spot."

The pharmacist's face is already braced.

Drink keeps going anyway. "I heard someone mention… Harrow Street. A little chemist near the park. The pharmacist there. Braid. Warm light."

The pharmacist blinks, and the smallest thing shifts. Not friendliness. Not permission. Recognition.

"That's not us," they say carefully.

"I know," Drink says. "That's the point."

A silence.

The pharmacist glances past him, toward the waiting area, toward the security guard's line of sight. They glance back at Drink. Take him in properly this time. His steady hands. His dry mouth. The ache in his face that isn't asking for a fix so much as asking for a direction.

Behind Drink, the queue keeps existing. Someone coughs into their sleeve. A receipt printer chatters. The injured worker limps up to the next window holding his script like proof of citizenship.

The pharmacist exhales through their nose.

"If you're looking for her," they say quietly, "you should go there. And you should go… calm."

Drink nods once, like he's receiving instructions for surgery.

"Thank you."

The pharmacist doesn't nod back like a blessing. They just turn slightly, already moving on, already swallowed by the next person's need.

Drink steps away.

His legs feel heavy, but they hold him.

He walks back through the waiting area, through the fluorescent corridor, through the smell that makes his skin crawl.

The security guard clocks him again and this time says nothing. The receptionist is on the phone, one hand covering the mouthpiece while she points a lost-looking man toward imaging. A printer spits out labels somewhere behind the desk. The cat carrier sits behind reception like a promise Drink is afraid to break.

The receptionist looks up as she hangs up the call. "That was quick."

Drink's laugh is a single breath that doesn't become a sound.

"Yeah," he says.

She slides the carrier back across the counter. The cat's eyes find Drink immediately. Accusation. Relief. Okay then.

Drink takes the handle gently.

"Thanks," he says, and means it in a way that surprises him.

The receptionist gives the kind of nod hospital workers give when they have already moved on internally but are still human enough to let you feel your gratitude.

Outside, the night hits his lungs like cold water.

The City is louder than before. Cars. Voices. Music leaking from a bar's open door. Warmth spilling out every time someone steps inside.

Drink's body angles toward it without permission.

He stops himself.

He looks down at his phone again.

He types Harrow Street into maps. A pin drops. The screen offers him a route as if it's nothing. As if this is ordinary.

As if he isn't about to walk toward the thing he has built into a myth.

He lifts the carrier slightly, readjusts the strap biting into his palm.

The cat shifts inside, unimpressed by the drama of humans. Alive. Heavy. Real.

A bar door opens halfway down the street.

Light spills across the pavement. Gold and warm. The sound of laughter rolls out with it, loose and careless. Someone inside shouts for another round. Glasses clink. Music thumps softly through the wall.

The smell reaches him a second later.

Beer. Sweet and bitter at the same time. The smell of a place where no one is waiting for anything except the next drink.

His body turns toward the light before his mind does. The movement is small, automatic, like a compass needle finding north.

He feels the first line of surrender arrive in him, not as language but as softness.

Just one.

Take the edge off.

No one would know in this part of town.

He stops walking.

The cat shifts again inside the carrier and lets out one low irritated sound, less a meow than a complaint.

Drink looks down.

Through the mesh, two eyes stare back at him with the flat patience of something that has no interest in symbolism and every interest in being carried somewhere safe.

Alive. Heavy. Real.

Drink stands there on the footpath with hospital air still clinging to his clothes and bar warmth touching only one side of his face.

Then he turns away from the door.

Not nobly. Not with triumph. Just by degrees. One shoulder. One foot. Then the rest.

The city is still moving when he reaches the cheap motel two streets over. The kind with tired carpet and a buzzing fluorescent light outside every door. He takes the room because it is late, and because tomorrow he will need to find Harrow Street.

Chapter Nine: The Invitation

Sober's friend texts her at breakfast.

The phone is face-down near the sugar bowl when it buzzes against the table, a small rude sound in an otherwise ordinary kitchen. Morning light sits pale on the bench. The kettle has only just clicked off. Outside the window, traffic is already moving, soft and constant, the city fully awake before she has properly decided whether she is.

She turns the phone over.

Dinner tonight?

Sober reads it twice.

The words are simple, but they carry the weight of choice. The temptation is not to go. To stay home. To keep life small until the past stops touching it.

She sits at the table in a T-shirt and old track pants, one foot tucked under the chair. Toast cools on a plate beside her. Tea steams in the mug she always reaches for first, the one with the handle glued once and holding so far. The apartment still carries sleep around the edges. Bed unmade. Curtain half open. The folded jumper still on the chair from two nights ago because there is no point pretending she is the kind of person who folds life neatly before work.

She thinks of the corporate representative's folder. Stability offered as relief. She thinks of the sick child's fevered head. She thinks of the teenager's cracked voice.

Her life is full already. Not empty.

That thought does not make the decision easier. Only clearer.

She types back:

Yes.

She watches the word sit there for a second before the message sends.

A pause. Then another message from her friend.

Good. Seven. Wear something you like.

Sober sets her phone down and stares at the kitchen wall as if it might offer a rule to follow. There isn't one.

The wall offers only what it always does. A small patch where the paint catches more light than the rest. A calendar hung slightly crooked. A grocery list held under a magnet shaped like a lemon. Dish soap still uncrossed from the list below bread and tea bags, both ticked days ago. Morning light moves across all of it without advice.

The kettle clicks as it cools.

Somewhere outside, a truck reverses with that patient bureaucratic beeping that makes every city sound temporarily industrial. In the flat above, something heavy scrapes once across the floor and then stops. Water moves through the pipes in the wall. A life stacked next to other lives.

Sober picks up her mug and drinks her tea before it has properly settled. It is too hot. She knows that before she does it anyway.

The invitation sits in her phone now like a task and not a threat.

That helps.

She eats half the toast standing at the sink. Butter gone cold. Crumbs in the basin. She rinses the plate immediately because she always does. The apartment is small enough that leaving one thing becomes leaving everything. The tap runs. The dish rack clinks softly. The city keeps moving beyond the window with no interest in her plans.

At work, the day behaves like a day.

That helps too.

A man comes in for antihistamines and says the wind is worse than the rain was. A school student buys pimple cream and gum. A woman in a blazer asks whether she stocks travel sickness tablets because her husband thinks ferries are romantic and she disagrees with her entire body. Sober answers, reaches, scans, bags.

The shop smells like hand cream and cardboard and the faint medicinal trace that lives in all pharmacies if you stand still long enough.

The door chime rings.

People come in with lunch breaks, with headaches, with toddlers, with exact change, with tired stories told only halfway. The shelves remain where she left them. The till balances. The day moves in units small enough to manage.

At one point her phone buzzes in the drawer under the counter.

She doesn't check it right away.

A regular customer is asking whether the new box is the same as the old box and needs to be shown the active ingredient in the same place as always. Then a courier arrives with stock. Then a child knocks over a small stand of tissues and stares at the damage as if grief has only just been invented. By the time she opens the drawer, the message has been sitting there ten minutes.

Just checking you're still coming :)

Her friend adds a second message before Sober can answer.

No pressure. Just food.

Sober smiles despite herself.

The smile is small and private. It disappears before the next customer steps up.

Still coming, she types.

Good, comes back almost immediately. I booked the little place near the tram stop.

Sober reads that twice too, not because the words are difficult, but because they push the evening into shape. A place. A time. A version of herself who turns up.

She puts the phone back in the drawer and closes it with her hip.

The rest of the shift is all ordinary friction.

A man in office clothes buys mints and hand sanitiser and asks whether she has aspirin loose in a smaller packet because he doesn't want to commit to the family size. A woman in activewear returns for the same expensive hand cream she bought last week and says it's either brilliant or she's becoming suggestible. Two schoolboys come in for lip balm and leave with lip balm, a protein bar, and a pack of plasters because one of them has managed to remove half the skin from his heel.

Somewhere between transactions, Sober becomes aware of the evening waiting for her.

Not ominously. Just there.

Like a coat hung by the door.

At six she flips the sign to CLOSED.

The motion is familiar enough to calm her.

The door locks. The till opens. Notes one stack, coins another. She writes the number down and checks it once. The fluorescent strips hum above her head. Out on the street, traffic has shifted into its early-evening rhythm, heavier but less hurried than morning.

She tidies without rushing.

Returns a bottle to the right shelf.

Straightens the lozenges.

Wipes the consult corner.

Checks that the scripts drawer is fully shut.

Routine makes the edges of things visible again.

In the back room, she takes off her apron and hangs it on the same hook she always uses. The room smells faintly of dust, cardboard, printer heat. One mug by the sink. A ledger on the table. The fridge humming with more loyalty than charm.

Her phone sits in her bag where she left it.

She looks at it and doesn't reach for it.

What she wears should not matter and still, apparently, does. That annoys her a little.

Back at the apartment, she stands in front of the wardrobe with the door open and feels faintly stupid.

The wardrobe is not dramatic. Two work dresses. Jeans. Shirts. A dark skirt she bought for a funeral and has worn twice since. A soft green top she likes and never quite believes on herself. Black boots. Flat shoes. A jacket that makes everything look deliberate whether she means it to or not.

Wear something you like.

The instruction is too open.

She reaches first for the safest option and stops.

Then for the most neutral and stops again.

The apartment holds its breath only in the sense that appliances do. The fridge hums. The A/C coughs once before settling into its steady quiet. A car horn sounds two streets over and is answered by nothing. Neighbours move behind walls. A drawer shuts upstairs. Water runs somewhere and stops.

Sober pulls the green top out.

Looks at it.

Puts it on the bed.

Chooses jeans. Then changes to the dark skirt. Then changes back to the jeans because she is not auditioning for her own life.

The whole process irritates her just enough to make her laugh once under her breath.

Not kindly. Not unkindly. Just accurately.

She dresses.

Washes her face.

Runs a brush through her hair and then decides against tying it back as tightly as she does for work. The looser version makes her look softer, which she notices and refuses to interpret. She puts on small earrings she forgot she owned. Not special ones. Just not everyday ones.

At the last minute she nearly changes back into her work shirt and doesn't.

That counts as something.

On the tram, the city is all movement and reflection.

Windows carry two versions of everything at once: shopfronts sliding by outside and tired passengers suspended over them in glass. A student with a saxophone case blocks half the aisle without meaning to. A woman in scrubs reads messages with the expression of someone still half at work. Two teenagers share chips from a paper bag and keep laughing at something one of them won't fully explain. The tram jerks, hums, stops, opens, closes.

Sober sits near the window and keeps one hand on her bag in her lap.

Her phone buzzes once.

We're out the back, her friend texts. *Blue jacket. Can't miss me.*

Outside, evening has turned the city soft in some places and harder in others.

Bars begin to fill. Office lights go dark floor by floor. A florist hoses down the footpath in front of closing buckets and bruised stems. A couple stand under an awning arguing quietly over whose turn it was to buy olive oil. A man in a suit eats sushi from a plastic tray while walking too fast to enjoy it.

The tram bell rings.

Sober gets off one stop early by habit and then decides not to fight that. The walk will do her good.

The restaurant is only three blocks away.

The street between is busy in the way good city streets are busy. Not dangerous. Not welcoming. Just occupied. People carrying bags. Phones. takeaway containers. children. their own weather. A woman in a red coat passes, talking into her headset about invoices. A cyclist swerves wide around a delivery rider. Somewhere behind her, glass is tipped into a bin with that hollow public sound of a venue resetting for the night.

She passes a bar with warm light and doesn't look in.

Not because she's afraid of what she'll see.

Because she doesn't need to.

She passes a chemist two streets over, bright and chain-owned and tidy in a way that never quite feels clean. A promotional sign in the window offers wellness points and half-price vitamins. She glances once and keeps going.

At the corner, she waits for the crossing signal beside a pram, a man in paint-splattered boots, and a young woman balancing flowers and a six-pack with surprising competence. The crossing beeps. They move. Mid-block a child on a scooter nearly clips her and calls "sorry" without slowing down. Sober steps aside and lets the moment go.

The restaurant is smaller than she expected.

A narrow front. Condensation on the windows. Handwritten specials on a board that has already been half erased for tomorrow. Inside, the tables are close enough to overhear but not so close you have to care. Warm light. Cutlery wrapped in napkins. A low drift of conversation and plates and kitchen clatter.

Her friend is at the back in a blue jacket, exactly as advertised.

She waves once, easy and visible.

Sober crosses the room with that small self-consciousness of entering somewhere other people are already settled.

Her friend stands just enough to hug her, then thinks better of making it a full event and turns it into a shoulder touch and a smile.

"You came."

Sober slides into the chair opposite. "I said I would."

"I know. Still."

The table is small, set for two, with a candle in a glass jar trying very hard not to look like a candle. Water sweats in a bottle between them. The menus are clipped to boards and smell faintly of laminated fingerprints.

A waiter appears with the expression of someone who can read a table's energy in under a second and respects it either way.

"Drinks?"

Her friend orders wine.

Sober almost says the same and stops.

The stop is brief. Invisible maybe. Still real.

"Mineral water," she says.

Her friend glances up, not surprised exactly, just noticing. Then she nods as if nothing about that choice needs naming.

"Same for me," she tells the waiter after a beat.

The waiter writes it down and disappears.

That small kindness lands harder than it should.

Sober looks at the menu to give her face somewhere to go.

Around them, the room keeps happening.

A couple by the window are deciding whether to split three dishes or over-order and be honest about it. Two men in shirtsleeves discuss someone named Darren who has apparently mismanaged a tender and now deserves whatever happens next. At the next table over, a family with one tired child and one very alert one are negotiating chips like a ceasefire agreement.

Her friend says, "You look tired."

Sober snorts softly. "Thank you."

"You know what I mean."

"I know."

The mineral water arrives in chilled glasses with slices of lemon that neither of them asked for. Condensation begins immediately. Her friend turns her glass once on the coaster and watches the water ring appear on the paper.

"How's the shop?"

"Busy."

"That good-busy or exhausting-busy?"

Sober considers.

"Both."

Her friend nods as if this was the expected answer. It probably was.

"Still no sale?"

Sober looks up.

The question is casual, but informed. Which means she must have mentioned the representative at some point. Maybe by text. Maybe in one of those half-conversations people have while checking on each other without ceremony.

"No sale," Sober says.

"Good."

The certainty in it makes Sober pause.

"Yeah?"

Her friend gives her a look over the top of the glass. "It's yours."

The sentence is simple enough to survive scrutiny.

Sober looks back at the menu though she isn't reading.

"It's also a lot."

"Those are allowed to both be true."

Sober smiles at that, a little despite herself.

The waiter comes back for their order. They choose without much drama. Pasta for one. Fish for the other. Bread to share because not sharing would make the table feel too earnest.

When the waiter leaves, her friend leans back and studies her for half a second in the way old friends do when they are deciding whether to open a door or leave it closed.

"You've been quieter."

Sober reaches for her water.

The glass is cold. The lemon smells bright and useless.

"It's been a week."

"That usually means something happened."

Sober looks at the candle in its glass jar. The flame is too small to matter and still insists on itself.

"A call," she says.

Her friend does not react theatrically.

That is one of the reasons Sober agreed to come.

Instead, she asks, "Bad?"

Sober thinks about that.

The landline at night.

The old fear arriving before the voice did.

The relief of hanging up first.

The way the apartment kept being an apartment afterward.

"Complicated," she says.

Her friend nods once.

They let that sit.

The bread arrives warm enough to steam when torn. Butter in a small dish. Olive oil that glows under the table light. They eat while the room goes on around them. A waiter drops a fork somewhere near the kitchen and mutters a fast apology to no one in particular. Someone at the bar laughs too loudly. A child asks whether prawns are bugs and receives a philosophical answer from a tired parent.

Her friend says, "Do you want to talk about it?"

Sober tears another piece of bread and watches the crumbs collect near her plate.

"Not really."

"Good," her friend says. "I wasn't fishing. Just checking."

That earns a real laugh from Sober this time.

Small, but real.

The food comes.

Steam. Plates warmed from the kitchen. Parsley trying hard. Lemon wedge. Pepper. The sort of meal that tastes better because someone else cooked it and brings it to you without asking what else needs doing.

They talk then about safer things.

A mutual acquaintance who has changed careers for the third time and still describes each shift like a calling.

A neighbour's ongoing war with a possum.

A pharmacist conference Sober has no intention of attending but will complain about anyway.

The conversation has enough lightness in it to feel earned rather than forced. It moves around the edges of heavier things without pretending they aren't there.

Halfway through, Sober realises she has unclenched her jaw.

Later, over the last of the water and the final shared piece of bread neither of them really wants but both eat, her friend says, "You know you're allowed to have a life that isn't just work and being brave."

Sober looks up.

The sentence could have been unbearable from the wrong person. Here, it lands softer.

She wipes a thumb over a breadcrumb on the table.

"I know."

"Do you?"

Sober thinks of the apartment. The shop. The route between. The phone on the counter. The choices that have become so practiced they sometimes pass for personality.

She thinks of the text that said Wear something you like.

Of standing in front of the wardrobe as if being seen casually was a harder task than most emergencies.

"Sometimes," she says.

Her friend nods like that is enough truth for one meal.

When they leave, the night has deepened.

The street outside is bright with restaurant spill and tram light and the reflective shine of recent washing on the footpaths. People stand in doorways talking with one shoulder turned toward home and the other still inside their night. A rideshare idles at the curb. Someone nearby is singing badly and with complete commitment.

They hug this time properly.

Not long. Just properly.

"Thanks," Sober says.

"For dinner?"

"For insisting."

Her friend smiles. "Any time."

They part at the corner.

Sober walks toward the tram stop with her jacket unbuttoned and her face still warm from the restaurant. The city moves around her in its ordinary way. A bar door opens. Laughter spills out. A tram rattles past already full. A couple argue quietly over directions. Someone drags a wheelie bin over uneven pavement, and the sound bounces off the buildings.

She checks her phone at the stop.

No new messages.

That is good.

Then, because she has trained herself into vigilance and not entirely out of it, she opens the thread with her friend again and rereads the first message.

Dinner tonight?

So little in the words. So much in having answered yes.

When the tram comes, she gets on.

The window gives her back a faint version of herself over the night city outside. Hair a little looser now. Mouth softer than it was this morning. Not transformed. Just slightly returned.

At home, she kicks off her shoes by the door and stands in the kitchen without turning on the television.

The apartment is quiet except for the A/C hum.

She fills a glass of water from the tap and drinks half of it in one go. Sets it down. Picks up her phone. Puts it down again.

The evening has not fixed anything.

That isn't the point.

The point, maybe, is smaller.

She went.

She wore something she liked.

She sat in a room that was not work and did not require rescue.

She let the night be only a night.

Before bed, she washes her face, hangs her jacket over the chair instead of putting it away, and checks the lock on the door with the same absent pressure she uses every night.

Then she turns off the lamp.

The room darkens.

The city continues.

And somewhere in it, without her needing to know where, the past keeps moving too.

Chapter Ten: Around the Corner

Drink wakes before his alarm, heart already running.

The cheap room's curtain glows faintly with dawn. Not sunlight exactly. Just the pale city version of morning, filtered through thin fabric and motel dust. The A/C hum hasn't stopped all night. The sound is both comfort and irritation, like a reminder that the world keeps working whether he deserves it or not.

The wall unit rattles once, settles, keeps going.

The room smells like stale air and old carpet and the detergent used on bedding that has belonged to too many strangers. There is a glass on the bedside table with a watermark dried into the bottom. His phone lies face-up beside it, alarm not yet due, screen dark. A chair in the corner holds yesterday's clothes in a shape that looks more surrendered than folded.

The cat is curled against his stomach, warm and heavy.

When Drink shifts, the cat opens one eye, blinks, and then closes it again, as if to say: stop making everything dramatic.

Drink lies still for a second longer, one hand resting lightly on the blanket near the cat's back. He can feel the small rise and fall of breathing through the fabric. It steadies nothing. It steadies something.

Then he sits up slowly.

His mouth is dry. His hands shake slightly. He holds them still by pressing his palms against the mattress. The springs give under his weight with a tired squeak. His body feels like it got no vote in any of this.

Today, he thinks, and the word is not hope, not dread. Just a date on a calendar. A series of hours.

He swings his legs over the side of the bed and waits for the room to settle around him.

Outside, a truck changes gears. Somewhere along the walkway outside the motel rooms, a door closes and someone drags a suitcase with one broken wheel. A television comes on in the room next door, volume low, morning news voices flattened by the wall.

Drink rubs both hands over his face and stands.

The cat stretches when he lifts him from the bed. Front paws long. Back arched. Claws briefly catching in the blanket. Drink sets him on the floor. The cat lands lightly, tail lifting, then pads to the door and sniffs under it with grave concentration.

The room smells like stale air and old carpet. The cat looks back at Drink as if asking why they're here.

Drink doesn't have a good answer.

He kneels by the carrier and unzips the side pocket where he stuffed the cat food last night. The kibble rattles into the small plastic bowl he bought at the discount shop. Dry, cheap, serviceable. The cat comes over without hurry and starts eating at once.

Drink watches, strangely soothed by the bluntness of the act.

Eat. Live. Move on.

The bowl knocks faintly against the lino each time the cat nudges it forward. Drink crouches there longer than he needs to, forearms resting on his knees, yesterday's shirt hanging open at the throat. The collar is still creased. He smells stale coffee in the fabric and the outside air he slept in.

He looks around the room as if something in it might tell him how to behave today.

A motel print bolted to the wall. Blue water. White sailboat. Nothing local enough to matter.

The small kettle on the bench with sachets of instant coffee and powdered milk laid out in rigid hospitality.

A Bible in the drawer he noticed last night and did not touch.

A mirror over the sink that makes the room look cleaner than it is from one angle and worse from another.

He turns on the tap. Water spits, then runs clear. He cups some into his mouth and swallows. Then again. He looks up into the mirror only because he has to.

He looks tired in a way that has stopped asking for sympathy.

Not ruined. Not heroic. Just badly slept.

He brushes his teeth with the motel sink light too bright above him. Foam. Cold porcelain. A drip from the tap he means to tighten and forgets. When he rinses, the sound seems too loud for the hour.

The cat finishes eating and licks one paw with insulting calm.

Drink packs the bowl away, folds the carrier flap back into place, checks his phone, checks it again as if the screen might show something new if he stares harder.

Nothing.

No message.

No correction.

No new fact.

He leaves the room with the carrier in one hand and yesterday's shirt still creased at the collar.

The corridor outside the rooms is concrete and paint and morning chill. A woman in a housekeeping polo pushes a trolley loaded with folded towels and tiny soaps in plastic wrappers. She glances at him, then at the carrier, then away again. Not judging. Just sorting him into the category of things she will not have to clean up if she's lucky.

The stair rail is cold under his palm.

In the car park, two men in work boots stand beside a ute drinking takeaway coffee from paper cups. One of them is explaining something with the same hand that holds a cigarette. The other nods without listening much. A magpie walks between white parking lines looking for something dropped and useful.

The morning air smells like damp concrete, petrol, and the first hot oil from the takeaway shop on the corner.

Drink shifts the carrier to his other hand.

The handle digs into his palm in the exact place it dug yesterday. The cat adjusts inside with a soft rustle and one brief complaint that doesn't rise to a full sound.

At the corner, outside a café opening for the morning, a woman in a volunteer vest steps into his path with a folded pamphlet already in her hand.

The café has only just pulled up its shutters. Chairs still upside down on half the tables. A boy in an apron hosing down the front step. A chalkboard sign leaning against the wall waiting to be taken outside. The smell of coffee is strong enough to feel like instruction.

The volunteer woman smiles with practiced urgency. Kind eyes. Tired face. Ponytail fraying out of its tie. The pamphlet is already halfway extended before she fully sees him.

"Shelter's two blocks over," she says. "They do breakfast."

Drink looks at her.

For a second he doesn't understand what she's seeing.

Then he does.

The carrier. The tired face. The cheap room behind him. Clothes worn twice. A man standing still with nowhere obvious to be.

"I'm not…" he says, and stops.

The woman blinks, the smile faltering but not collapsing.

"Sorry," she says quickly. "I just thought…"

Drink shakes his head once.

"It's alright."

And it is, mostly, except for the way the moment lands in him.

Not insult.

Recognition from the wrong angle.

The woman pulls the pamphlet back toward herself, folds it once more along a line that already exists. "They're good people," she says, as if she needs to save the interaction from becoming shame.

Drink nods. "Okay."

She nods back and moves on toward a man sleeping half upright on the bench near the bus stop, this time slower, more certain.

Drink stands there one beat too long.

The café boy carries the chalkboard out onto the footpath. Fresh muffins. $5.50 coffees. Bacon and egg roll special. The black text is still damp enough to shine. A customer in office clothes ducks inside while buttoning his cuff. A cyclist in a helmet asks whether they're doing oat milk yet. The day opens around Drink without waiting for him to decide what the moment means.

He walks.

The cat carrier bumps gently against his leg in time with his steps.

The suburb changes by small degrees as he goes. Motels and discount stores first. Then a hardware place with roller doors already up, the smell of cut timber drifting out. The kind of place he works in now. Then a florist dragging buckets onto the footpath. Then narrower streets where the trees have been left in place because someone once cared what that looked like.

The city is waking in layers.

School uniforms.

Delivery vans.

A man jogging with bad form and expensive shoes.

A woman smoking in slippers outside an apartment block while scrolling her phone with one hand.

A bakery window filling with pastries behind the glass.

At a crossing, Drink stops beside an older man carrying a plastic bag of apples and a kid in headphones kicking at the pole base while he waits for the light to change. The crossing beeps. They move. No one looks at him long enough to decide anything.

He follows the map on his phone, though by now he doesn't need it every second.

Harrow Street.

Around the park.

The warm little chemist.

Each piece of direction has become heavier through repetition.

When the first glimpse of the park appears between buildings, his chest tightens.

It is smaller than he imagined and more ordinary. Grass. A low fence. A slide. A couple of benches. A streetlight near one end. Trees that are trying hard in city soil.

He slows.

Around the corner from the park, the pharmacy sits exactly where a person might miss it if they weren't looking. Narrow frontage. Warm interior light not yet fully visible in the morning brightness. A hand-painted sign with the gold worn a little at the edges. Not shabby. Kept.

Not curated like the apothecary. Not efficient like the chain. Not institutional like the hospital.

Human.

Drink stops half a block away.

A bus passes between him and the window. When it clears, the shop is still there.

He shifts the carrier down to the pavement and flexes his fingers. The strap has marked his skin red. Through the mesh, the cat's face appears and then disappears again as he repositions himself.

Drink does not move closer immediately.

A woman with a pram comes out of the chemist holding a small paper bag folded neatly at the top. She pauses to adjust the blanket over the baby's legs, then keeps going. A man in a council polo walks in carrying a script folded lengthwise in one hand and talking on his phone with the other. Through the glass, a figure moves behind the counter and disappears down an aisle.

Warm light. Shelves. The shape of a place that still belongs to itself.

Drink picks up the carrier again and crosses the street.

The bell above the door gives a small sound when he enters.

Inside, the shop smells like hand cream and cardboard and the faint clean bitterness of real pharmacy stock. Fluorescent light hums overhead, but warmer bulbs near the counter soften it. The effect is practical first, pleasant second. A narrow aisle of vitamins. Shelves of baby products. Pain relief. Tissues. Soap. A rack of greeting cards no one has updated in too long.

He stands just inside the door.

The carrier rests against his shin.

Near the counter, a teenager in school uniform pays for a drink and a packet of gum. The EFTPOS machine chirps. The girl shoves both items into her bag and leaves without looking up. Behind her, an elderly man waits with a script and a kind of patient impatience that suggests he has been waiting for systems all his life and dislikes none of them individually.

Drink looks toward the counter.

He doesn't see Sober.

Not at first.

A younger staff member in navy scrubs is taping up a paper bag behind the till. A nametag on the pocket reads *Maya.* Someone else passes through a half-open doorway toward the dispensary at the back. Drink's heart is already running ahead of facts.

He moves to one side and pretends to study a shelf of cold-and-flu tablets.

The boxes line up in bright colours designed to simplify misery. *Day. Night. Max. Relief. Mucus. Cough. Sinus.* He reads none of it.

A toddler near the nappy aisle is hitting a packet of wipes against the lower shelf in a rhythm only toddlers understand. His father kneels beside him comparing two creams with the seriousness of treaty negotiation. An older woman in a cardigan asks the staff member whether the generic is really the same or whether they only say that because they have to.

The shop is alive in the way small useful places are alive. Not loud. Not quiet. A braid of need and repetition.

Drink waits for a gap that never quite comes.

That, more than anything, tells him this is her place.

Not ownership necessarily. But gravity.

A regular rhythm.

The older man at the counter unfolds and refolds his script while the staff member explains a dosage change. The toddler loses interest in the wipes and wants the floor now. The father says no in the flat calm tone of someone saying no for the forty-fifth time today.

Then a woman steps out from the dispensary door with a tray of boxes in both hands.

Hair tied back.

A braid resting between her shoulders.

Plain blouse. Practical shoes. Name badge catching light when she turns.

Sober.

The sight of her does not hit him like revelation.

It is worse than that.

It is recognition.

Immediate and bodily and unspectacular. Like seeing your own street after being lost.

Drink goes very still.

She does not see him. Not yet.

She sets the tray on the back bench, picks up one box, checks the label, speaks quietly to the younger staff member, then turns toward the shelf behind the counter and slots the box into place with the economy of someone who has done this movement ten thousand times.

No music changes. Nothing in the room marks the moment except the fact that Drink can suddenly hear his own breathing too clearly.

He grips the carrier handle harder than he means to. The cat shifts inside and gives one annoyed sound. Not loud. Enough.

Sober glances toward the noise.

Their eyes meet.

No one around them notices immediately.

The father is still negotiating creams. The older woman is asking whether cod liver oil has changed brands. Outside, a truck brakes hard at the lights and the sound comes dimly through the glass.

Sober doesn't drop anything. She doesn't go pale. She doesn't step toward him.

She just stops moving for one second.

Then starts again.

Not because she hasn't seen him.

Because there are customers.

Because the day is already in progress.

Because a life kept going.

Drink feels shame and relief arrive together so fast they make him light-headed.

He does not step forward.

He does not say her name across the counter.

Sober looks at the carrier, then back at him, then at the older man waiting for his packet.

"Just a moment," she says to the man, and the sentence is so ordinary it almost undoes him.

The man nods as if there is nothing in the room more important than his blood pressure tablets and his Wednesday routine.

Drink stands by the cold-and-flu shelf with the carrier at his feet and waits to be asked into whatever this is.

Sober says something low to the younger staff member, who glances over once, quickly, and then nods.

She finishes with the older man first.

That matters.

Drink sees that it matters and hates himself for having wanted, even for a moment, not to come second to ordinary need.

The transaction completes. Paper bag folded. Quiet thanks. The older man leaves.

The father takes his creams and a packet of teething gel he did not intend to buy. The toddler begins crying because the crying had to happen somewhere. The door opens. Closes. The shop thins.

Sober comes around from behind the counter.

Not quickly.

Not slowly.

Just with intent.

She stops a few feet from him, close enough to make this real, far enough to keep it hers.

Drink opens his mouth.

Nothing useful arrives.

Sober's eyes move over him once. The tired shirt. The carrier. The dry face. The hands held too carefully at his sides.

Then she says, in the same voice she would use to ask after dosage or timing or whether someone had eaten today:

"You found it."

Drink nods once.

Sober glances toward the counter where Maya is folding receipts.

"Not here," she says quietly.

She tears a scrap from a prescription pad and writes something on it.

"Park," she says. "Noon. Bench by the streetlight."

Chapter Eleven: Park Bench

Drink folds the scrap from the prescription pad once and puts it in his wallet, though he does not need to.

Park. Noon. Bench by the streetlight.

He steps back out onto Harrow Street with the carrier in one hand and the taste of the shop still in his mouth. Hand cream. Cardboard. Ordinary need continuing without him.

The park sits where it sat all morning. Small. Functional. Not picturesque enough to turn into meaning without effort. A slide. Two benches. The streetlight. A low fence near the path. A council bin with peeling stickers. Someone has tied a faded blue ribbon to one of the rails and left it there long enough for weather to make it anonymous.

He does not go in straight away.

He stands under the nearest tree and watches the path as if the extra minute might teach him how to do this cleanly. A woman walks a stocky brown dog past the park entrance. The dog stops at the base of the tree and refuses to move until it has finished whatever private investigation it has begun. Two boys kick a football too hard in the grass and one of them has to run after it before it reaches the road. A cyclist rings a bell toward no one in particular and threads between a pram and a man carrying takeaway coffees.

Drink keeps one hand on the carrier handle without gripping it.

His chest aches with wanting.

Not just wanting her.

Wanting the quiet that comes after.

At a corner kiosk, he buys two coffees he already knows he shouldn't.

The kiosk is wedged between a florist and a tobacconist, all chrome surfaces and a cash drawer that sticks out a centimetre before opening properly. The espresso machine hisses and knocks and lets out bursts of steam. Behind Drink, a woman in office clothes orders oat milk and extra hot without looking up from her phone. A delivery rider waits with his helmet under one arm and checks the road every five seconds like impatience might change traffic.

"What size?" the barista asks.

Drink glances at the menu board and realises he hasn't thought that far.

"Regular."

"Two?"

"Yeah."

The barista fills the cups, snaps lids into place, and writes nothing on them because there is nothing to distinguish one from the other except the fact that one of them might not be touched. Drink taps his card. Approved. The little machine chirps once. He picks up the cardboard tray with one hand and steadies it before turning away.

He carries the coffees carefully, as if steadiness is something you practise.

At the park, a streetlight stands at the edge of a bench. The bench faces the road. Cars pass in constant motion. People walk dogs. A jogger runs by with earphones in. Life continues around the quiet centre of the bench.

Drink arrives early. He sits. He sets the coffees beside him. The cat carrier rests at his feet. The cat inside shifts, alert, eyes wide.

He waits.

The bench is painted green in theory and mostly worn back to metal in practice. The slats press into the backs of his legs. The streetlight pole beside him is tagged near the base with silver marker, letters too stylised to be read. A bus goes past close enough to shake the bench a fraction. Drink watches it pull away and notices his own reflection in the window for half a second, blurred and accidental.

He listens to the traffic hum. He watches the shadows move slightly as clouds pass.

A man with a pram stops near the fence to answer a call and says, “No, mate, I’m with her now,” in the tone of someone trying to prove a thing by saying it louder. A runner stretches one calf against the streetlight and then moves on. A magpie lands on the grass, head tilted, then hops away when the cat shifts in the carrier.

Drink lifts one coffee, sips, and sets it back down.

Bitter, hot, grounding.

His mind races through apologies, explanations, vows. He pushes them away. Apologies can be weapons if they are used to ask for something in return.

He tries to think only in instructions.

Stay seated.

Don’t stand too fast.

Don’t reach for her.

Don’t talk over silence.

A car stereo at the lights sends a soft pulse of bass into the park, then the lights change and it’s gone. Somewhere behind him a child starts crying over some ordinary catastrophe and is talked down by an exhausted parent. The second coffee cools by degrees in its cup, lid gathering a sheen of steam.

At noon, footsteps approach on the path behind him. He doesn't turn right away. He feels the presence before he sees it, like heat behind his neck.

Then he turns.

And there she is.

Sober.

Not the woman he saw in the chemist. Not the voice through a landline at midnight. Not the remembered version. Not the girl under the school tree or the woman beside him in the registry office. Just Sober, here, in daylight, standing by a public bench with traffic moving behind her.

She has dressed for the day rather than for him. Coat buttoned over her uniform. Hair tied back. Shoes made for walking rather than ceremony. One hand still near her bag strap as if she has only just stopped moving. Her face is calm in the worked-for way calm sometimes is.

For a second neither of them speaks.

The pause is not cinematic. A dog barks across the road. A tram bell sounds from farther up the street. A bus stop advertisement behind her promises effortless connection in large cheerful font.

Drink stands too quickly, then catches himself and stops halfway to momentum.

Sober glances once at the second coffee and then at the carrier.

He follows her gaze.

"I didn't know if you'd want one," he says.

The sentence sounds foolish as soon as it leaves him.

Sober looks back at him. Not cruel. Not softened into rescue either.

Then she says, "Sit."

He sits.

She takes the other end of the bench, leaving enough space for the space to matter. Not theatrical distance. Not intimacy. A clear amount of public bench between them.

The carrier stays at Drink's feet. The cat watches through the mesh with the flat patience of something already resigned to human weather.

Sober does not touch the coffee.

Cars pass. A cyclist slows at the crossing. A child in a yellow hat drops a cracker and bursts into tears as if the world has personally betrayed him. His mother picks it up, throws it away, produces another from a plastic container, and the crisis ends.

Drink keeps his hands around his own cup because they need somewhere to go.

Sober looks at the road for a moment before looking at him.

"You look tired."

He lets out a breath that almost becomes a laugh and doesn't.

"Yeah."

Neither of them reaches for the larger sentences waiting behind the smaller one.

The coffee in his hand has already cooled enough to drink properly. He doesn't.

Sober's eyes move once over his face. Not examining. Registering.

Then to the carrier again. "You brought him."

Drink glances down.

The cat blinks back, unimpressed.

"Yeah."

A pause.

"He's alright?"

Drink nods. "He's been better than me."

Sober's mouth changes slightly at that. Not a smile exactly. The memory of how one might start.

She bends one hand around the edge of the bench slat beside her. Fingers resting. Not clenched.

Traffic keeps moving. A council truck goes past with two workers inside talking to each other and not looking out. A woman in a corporate lanyard power-walks around the park while eating something from a small tub with a plastic fork. A crow pecks at a chip wrapper under the other bench and gives up.

Drink looks at Sober and then at the road and then back again.

There are too many true things.

They crowd each other out.

He picks one that does not ask for anything.

"Thanks for coming."

Sober nods once.

"I said noon."

It is not a joke. Not exactly. But it has the shape of one.

Drink swallows. "Yeah."

Another pause.

The second coffee sits untouched between them, steam almost gone now.

Sober notices it again. "You shouldn't have done that."

Drink nods. "I know."

He does know. It was not a gift exactly, but it leaned in that direction. An offering. A version of trying too hard shaped like takeaway cups.

He reaches over, picks it up, and sets it on the ground beside the bench instead of between them.

That small correction seems to help.

For a while they sit with the road in front of them and the path behind.

Drink can feel every old instinct trying to crowd in.

Explain.

Promise.

Prove.

Sober sits inside the same silence without rescuing him from it.

That matters too.

When she speaks again, it is with the same practical tone she used in the shop.

"You found the place."

Drink nods.

"Hospital."

The answer sounds absurdly simple.

Sober looks ahead. "Of course."

He risks a glance at her. "Thank you for meeting with me."

"Why are you here?"

A jogger passes behind them with breath loud in his headphones. A small dog stops at the carrier and sniffs with great seriousness until its owner tugs it away, apologising to no one in particular. The cat remains still, only his tail giving one slow movement inside the mesh.

Drink says, "I'm not here to ask you for anything."

Sober turns her head then and looks at him properly.

It is not disbelief.

It is assessment.

The kind she gives labels and doses and customers who insist they're fine while sweating through their shirt.

Drink holds the look as long as he can.

Then looks down at the seam in his jeans.

"I know how that sounds," he says.

Sober's voice stays even. "Do you?"

He nods once.

The answer could become a larger fight if either of them pushed it. It doesn't. A bus shelters at the lights. A teenager on a scooter nearly collides with the pole and swears softly at himself. Somewhere nearby a bottle tips into a public bin with that hollow municipal sound that always carries farther than it should.

Drink lifts his coffee, takes a sip, burns his tongue slightly because he forgot it was still hot in the centre. The pain steadies him.

"I just wanted to say I'm sorry," he says. "Without making that your job."

Sober keeps watching him.

A long enough silence that he almost ruins it by adding more.

Then she says, "Good."

The word is not absolution. It is a permission to continue if he can do it cleanly.

He nods.

The park breathes around them.

A kid on the slide shouts, "Again," with the certainty of someone who still believes the world is built to repeat pleasure on request. His father climbs the steps behind him looking wrecked already. A woman in activewear drops her keys, swears under her breath, and laughs at herself before anyone else can.

Drink says, "I was going to say a lot more."

Sober's gaze shifts back to the road. "I assumed so."

That almost gets a real laugh out of him.

Almost.

"I cut most of it."

"Good."

He rubs his thumb against the paper cup seam.

"There were a lot of versions where I sounded better than I was."

Sober says nothing.

"That didn't seem fair."

A silence again. Not empty. Working.

Then Sober says, "No."

He looks at her, startled not by the word but by how quickly she understood what he meant.

The second coffee on the ground beside the bench is cooling into irrelevance.

Drink says, "I'm sober."

The sentence arrives plain. No fanfare. No badge. No claim attached.

Sober's face does not change much, but something in it settles a fraction lower, closer to pain than surprise.

"How long?"

He tells her.

Not because the number proves anything.

Because she asked.

She nods once.

Again, no congratulations. No reward.

The rule of the world holds.

Drink feels the absence of reward like a structure he can finally lean on.

"I know that doesn't…" He stops. Starts again. "I know."

Sober folds and unfolds one corner of a tissue she has taken from her bag without using it.

"I'm glad," she says.

That is all.

It is not small, exactly. But it is exact.

Drink closes his eyes for half a second, then opens them again.

Traffic moves. A tram rattles past. The shadow of the streetlight shifts by degrees across the path. A man in a council vest empties the bin near the gate and wheels it away without ever looking at the bench.

Sober's hand comes to rest lightly on the top of the carrier.

"He stayed with you."

Drink looks down at the mesh. "Yeah."

The cat shifts once, then settles again under his hand.

Sober keeps her eyes there a second longer than she means to.

"We tried for years."

The words come out flat. Not dramatic. A fact. They sit between them like the bench.

Drink's jaw tightens. His eyes shine, but he does not cry.

"It wasn't anyone's fault."

Traffic moves through the intersection. A tram bell sounds. Somewhere behind them a child laughs too hard at something small.

Drink looks at his hands. "I didn't know how to be in it."

Sober nods once. She does not argue with the sentence. She lets it stand.

She turns and looks at him properly.

"I had to forgive myself too."

His face changes slightly. "For what?"

"For thinking love would be enough," she says. "For staying too long. For leaving too late. For making my life revolve around whether you were okay."

The tissue in her hand has softened at the corner from being turned over and over.

"You need more than I can give."

Drink closes his eyes for a second. When he opens them, they look tired rather than startled.

"I know."

This time she believes him.

The cat makes a small sound inside the carrier and noses at the zip.

Drink bends and opens it a little.

The cat's head appears. Bright eyes. Serious whiskers.

Sober leans forward before she can stop herself and offers two fingers.

The cat sniffs them. Then presses his head into her hand.

"Hi, you."

The words come out soft and unplanned.

Her throat tightens.

Drink watches the cat with an attention that looks almost painful.

The cat climbs halfway out, paws on Drink's knee, pauses, looks at Sober, then settles back against Drink's leg with quiet certainty.

Sober feels the choice like a small knife.

"He chose."

Drink's hand trembles once as he strokes the cat's head.

Sober lets out a slow breath.

"Keep him."

Drink looks up. "I…"

"Keep him," she says again, not harshly. Just clearly.

He nods.

A child goes past on a scooter, chanting a playground rhyme to a boy and girl playing in the sandpit together.

Drink catches the beginning.

"Felix and Emma sitting in a tree."

The child's voice drifts on as he circles the path.

"K.I.S.S.I.N.G."

Then, thinner with distance:

"First comes love."

"Then comes marriage."

A bus pulls up at the lights. Doors sigh open. Someone coughs. By the time the traffic clears, the last line has already gone.

Sober stands.

Drink stands too, slower this time, careful not to jostle the carrier.

For the first time that day she steps fully into his space and wraps her arms around him.

It is brief. Gentle. A goodbye with tenderness.

He holds her like something that cannot be owned.

When she steps back, the air between them returns.

"Stay on your path."

"I will."

She steadies her mouth.

"For you."

Drink swallows. "For me."

Then she turns and walks south along the path, toward the tram stop and the city beyond it.

Drink stays where he is.

He watches her go without calling after her.

That is part of the meeting too.

The park keeps happening.

A council worker drags a blower from the maintenance shed and starts pushing leaves in a direction leaves do not especially respect. The father from earlier finally sits on the edge of the slide platform while his kid climbs back up again. A cyclist pauses at the crossing and drinks water from a bottle without getting off the bike.

Drink does not sit immediately.

He stands with the carrier in one hand and the cooling coffee in the other and lets the fact of the meeting settle into him without turning it into a lesson too quickly.

Eventually he bends, picks up the untouched coffee from beside the bench, and carries both cups to the bin.

He throws them away.

The plastic lids knock softly against the side.

No ceremony.

He returns to the bench and sits again because his legs are not ready to move yet.

The cat shifts in the carrier, then settles. Drink places the carrier gently beside him on the bench this time, unzipping the top just enough for air and a hand. The cat does not come out. He only pushes his head once against Drink's fingers and then remains where he is.

Cars pass. A tram rings. Someone nearby unwraps chips.

The bench feels like any bench again.

That is the hardest part maybe. Not that the moment was large. That it has already returned to public furniture and traffic and a park by a road.

Drink sits through that too.

After a while, his phone buzzes.

A message from his sponsor.

How'd it go?

Drink looks at the words.

Looks at the road.

Looks at the carrier.

Then types the cleanest answer he has.

We talked. She left.

He sends it.

The reply takes a minute.

Good.

At first the word stings. Then it doesn't.

Of course good.

Not because it feels good.

Because the truth happened and no one turned it into theatre.

Drink locks the phone and pockets it.

He sits another minute.

Then another.

When he finally stands, he does not look south again.

He picks up the carrier and starts walking north.

The city receives him the same way it received everyone else.

No music.

No verdict.

Just traffic, weather, people, and the next ordinary task.

Epilogue: Tomorrow

The next morning, Sober opens the shop.

The key turns in the lock with a small resistant click before giving way. The door sticks for half a second in the frame, swollen slightly from weather, and she shoulders it open with her bag still on. Cool morning air comes in with her, carrying the smell of damp pavement and traffic that has already committed to the day.

The shop is dim when she enters.

Shelves in outline. Counter in shadow. The faint shape of the consult corner. The familiar waiting body of the place before it becomes itself.

She flicks on the lights row by row.

The door chime rings. The fluorescent hum steadies. The city moves outside the glass.

The first strip catches and then holds. The second comes on cleanly. Boxes emerge from shadow. Labels. Price tags.

The till. The hand sanitiser bottle on the counter. The small bowl near the register with travel tissues and lip balm no one comes in for but people always add.

She sets her bag down in the back room, comes out again, and straightens a display that does not need straightening. Pulls the till drawer open. Counts the float. Notes in one stack, coins in another. The metal sounds of them are small and practical.

Outside, a delivery van idles in the loading zone too long. A cyclist rings a bell and passes a pram by inches. Across the street, the bakery lifts its shutters and warm bread smell reaches the footpath in brief soft waves whenever the wind moves the right way.

She greets a regular and smiles, brief and real.

He comes in for the same blood pressure tablets he always collects on Tuesdays, folded script in one hand though he no longer needs to bring it. He comments on the weather without fully committing to an opinion on it. She scans the box, bags it, tells him to have a good day. He nods as if this exchange matters exactly as much as it should.

A woman in activewear asks where the magnesium is.

A parent wants children's paracetamol and tissues.

A teenager lingers by the pimple cream until Sober steps closer and taps the right shelf without making a speech.

The shop fills and empties in ordinary measures.

The door opens. Closes.

Receipts print.

The fridge hum from the back room comes and goes beneath it all.

Her phone stays in her bag. The landline stays quiet.

It sits on the counter where it always sits, cream plastic gone slightly yellow with age, the cord curled into its own memory. Morning light from the front window catches one edge of it and then moves on. She does not touch it except once to shift it an inch so she can wipe beneath.

When she catches herself thinking of the park bench, she lets the thought pass like traffic noise. Not denial. Not obsession. Just a memory moving through.

The bench under the streetlight. The second untouched coffee. Drink's tired face. The carrier at his feet. Sober does not push the memory away. She does not sit inside it either. It arrives, changes the light in the room for half a second, then keeps moving.

A customer asks whether the generic is the same and she answers.

A toddler drops a drink bottle and it rolls under the shelving.

Someone laughs outside at something she cannot hear.

The day continues because it was always going to.

At midday, she steps into the back room and drinks a glass of water.

The room is cool in the unwelcoming way storage rooms are cool. Stock boxes stacked by brand and size. One mug near the sink. A tea towel hanging off the cupboard handle. The water from the tap is colder than she expects and tastes faintly metallic through the glass.

The fridge hums. The ledger sits open.

The page is ruled with numbers and notes in her own neat hand. An order to place. A stock item running low. A reminder to chase an invoice that should have been paid already. The small spine of a business. Nothing noble in it. Nothing theatrical. Just the work required to keep the lights on and the shelves stocked and the room functioning when people arrive needing things.

Her life has edges. She is grateful for them.

Not grateful in a grand way.

Not as revelation.

Just in the bodily sense of being able to stand inside a day and know what belongs to her and what does not.

She rinses the glass as soon as she finishes. Sets it upside down on the drying mat. Wipes one drop of water from the bench with the side of her hand. Then she goes back out.

Across the city, Drink sits in a meeting room under fluorescent light.

The building smells faintly of old carpet, instant coffee, and rain drying on coats. The chairs are metal-framed with vinyl seats that keep the cold in them no matter how long the room has been occupied. A heater clicks in one corner and contributes almost nothing. Someone has set out paper cups in uneven stacks beside a tin of coffee and a plastic tub of sugar sachets.

Metal chairs scrape. Coffee smells burnt. People say their names in tired voices.

A man in hi-vis rubs one knee while he listens. A woman in office clothes keeps both hands around a paper cup gone lukewarm. Another man stares at the floor until it's his turn and then looks up only as long as he has to. The posters on the wall curl at the corners. A crisis number. A tenancy service. A flyer about volunteering no one is reading.

Drink sits with the cat carrier at his feet.

The cat has gone still inside it, settled into that particular patience animals have when they've stopped expecting to understand the logic of human rooms.

Drink's coffee sits untouched on the floor beside his chair until it cools enough to stop steaming.

Drink speaks when it's his turn. His voice is rough. It holds.

He does not make it larger than it is.

He says his name.

He says enough.

The room takes it without applause.

Someone nods once from across the circle. Someone else tears open a sugar sachet with their teeth. A cup is set down on the lino with a tiny sound that carries farther than it should.

The fluorescent hum stays steady above all of it.

After the meeting, his phone buzzes.

People stand in small clusters after the formal part ends. Not friends, not strangers exactly. Just people who have seen enough of each other to say goodbye without pretending they know what comes next. A man rinses two mugs at the sink. Someone folds up chairs from the spare stack against the wall. The room begins returning to community-centre neutral.

Drink steps into the corridor before checking the message.

The hallway smells like floor cleaner and old paint. A vending machine at the far end throws blue light into the dullness. Through a half-open door nearby, someone in another room is stacking plastic trestle tables. The building keeps reassigning itself.

You alright, tonight?

Drink looks at the message and feels the familiar urge to avoid.

To let silence answer for him.

To believe one difficult truth has somehow earned him a day off from the next one.

Then he feels the cat's carrier handle in his hand, the cat's steady weight inside, the memory of the streetlight buzz and Sober's voice, plain and final.

None of it comforts him exactly.

That is not what steadiness is.

The carrier handle digs into the same place in his palm it always does. The cat shifts once inside with a quiet scrape against fabric. Somewhere outside, traffic moves over wet road with that soft continual hiss cities make when they don't care what anyone has learned.

He types one word.

Yeah.

He sends it.

The message goes. No fanfare. No relief music. Just the small digital certainty of a thing done.

The city keeps moving.

Buses kneel and rise at curbs.

Shop doors open and close.

Receipts print.

Kettles click off.

Streetlights wait for evening.

The hum of machines fills rooms where people sleep.

Air conditioners.

Fridges.

Vending machines.

Hospital vents.

The low electric breath of buildings keeping themselves going through the night and into whatever comes next.

Life continues. Not as reward. As fact.

The End.

Samfa12

www.ingramcontent.com/pod-product-compliance
Lightning Source LLC
LaVergne TN
LVHW030921080826
845145LV00013B/2992

* 9 7 8 1 7 6 4 6 3 8 4 0 1 *